"Have you ever cried for him, Luke?"

"What do you think it will prove? You think that if I *cry* for Dan, I won't feel like someone has yanked out half my guts? It doesn't work that way, sweetheart!"

"Don't you patronize me, Lucas Brand! I'm not your 'sweetheart,' I'm your friend, and I deserve a little respect from you."

When the word *friend* came out of her mouth, Luke felt his stomach clench. No matter how many times he told himself to think of her that way, he couldn't. Even now, when she was ticking him off beyond belief, he wanted her. His body ached for her.

She was everything he wanted in a woman: strong, independent, incredibly smart and sexier now than she had ever been.

He wanted to kiss the breath right out of her, until the word *friend* was permanently eradicated from her brain. But, whenever he came close to crossing that line, Luke would look down at her belly, and that would stop him cold.

Dear Reader,

When I was twelve years old, my family spent the summer on a working Montana cattle ranch. I remember that I loved the ranch so much that I cried when I had to return to my home in Florida. I have never forgotten the magic of Montana's pristine mountains and the seemingly endless blue sky. When it was time to pick a setting for *A Baby For Christmas,* I couldn't imagine a better place than a Montana ranch. And the ranch house of my childhood memories was never far from my mind when I created the Brand family home at Bent Tree as the backdrop for Luke and Sophia's love story.

For me, writing for Harlequin is a lifelong dream that actually came true. I hope that *A Baby For Christmas* is the first of many stories featuring the Brand Clan and I hope that you enjoy spending time with Luke and Sophia as much as I have.

Happy holidays!

Joanna

A BABY FOR CHRISTMAS

JOANNA SIMS

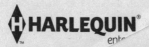

⬥ **HARLEQUIN**®
ente

Recycling programs
for this product may
not exist in your area.

ISBN-13: 978-0-373-65714-8

A BABY FOR CHRISTMAS

This edition published by arrangement with Harlequin Books S.A.

For questions and comments about the quality of this book, please contact us at CustomerService@Harlequin.com.

™ are trademarks of Harlequin Enterprises Limited or its corporate www.trademarks indicated with ® are registered in the United States Patent Office, the Canadian Trade Marks Office and in other countries.

Printed in U.S.A.

Books by Joanna Sims

Harlequin Special Edition

A Baby For Christmas #2232

JOANNA SIMS

lives in Florida with her husband and their three fabulous felines. Joanna works as a therapist for the public school system during the day, but spends her evenings and weekends fulfilling her lifelong dream of writing compelling, modern romances for Harlequin Books. When it's time to take a break from writing, Joanna enjoys going for long walks with her husband and curling up on the couch to watch movies (romantic comedies preferably). She loves to answer any questions or provide additional information for her readers. You can contact her at Joannasims2@live.com.

Dedicated to my husband, Cory
You are the true love of my life

Chapter One

Captain Luke Brand was home for the holidays. Against his will. As far as he was concerned, First Recon was still in Afghanistan, so *he* should still be in Afghanistan. Bottom line. And it didn't matter that an insurgent had blown a bullet clean through his left leg. It didn't matter to him that he had almost lost the leg. *Almost* didn't count. His leg was still attached; he should return to active duty. But the Marines sure as hell didn't see it that way. They denied his request, patched him up and shipped his butt back to the States for medical leave. Like it or not, he was on his way home.

And he didn't like it. Not by a long shot.

The military had gotten him as far as Helena; now Billy Whiteside, an old high school buddy, was taking him the rest of the way to his family's Montana ranch. Bent Tree was less than an hour away. Luke wished it were two hours. Three would be even better. He wasn't in a hurry to tangle with his sister-in-law, Sophia; from his point of view, fighting the Taliban for control of Afghan towns seemed like a much easier task.

"He's found a good spot to hang out." Billy glanced over at the black kitten perched on Luke's left leg. Luke looked down at the scrawny kitten and grunted in response. The kitten had started the trip in a box situated between Billy and Luke. Once the kitten caught Luke's eye, he made a determined escape from the box, and a beeline for Luke's leg. Luke had always liked an underdog, and this kitten certainly qualified; found in a ball of toilet paper in a truck stop restroom, half starved, half frozen. He was lucky to be alive. He was a survivor. Luke liked that about him. So, when the kitten had gingerly sat down on the exact spot where his leg was wounded, Luke didn't have the heart to make him move. In fact, the warmth of the kitten's body and the vibrations of his purr seemed to ease the pain a bit.

"He's lucky he didn't end up in the Dumpster...." Billy's naturally round face had gotten even rounder with weight and age; he still easily wore a giant grin that split his face. Billy reached over and banged on the dashboard of his Chevy to get the heater kicked on again. "Cindy swept him right up into the dustpan. Can you believe *that?* 'Course, she didn't know what was in that mess'a paper. How could she know, ya know? 'Course, Cindy can't keep him. What with four kids, two dogs, a couple of cats and that pig her youngest is raisin'! And, I don't know, man... I think my ol' lady will put me out in the barn if I bring anything else home. But what else could I do? I couldn't just leave him there..." Billy banged on the dash again. "And, it looks like he picked you... Cats pick their owners, you know. Didn't you tell me that? No! It was your mom who told me that! Your mom told me that...."

Luke didn't bother to reply. He knew what Billy was getting at. He was trying to pawn this scruffy orphan off on him. Not a chance! The little fur ball would just have to go back into the box when the ride was over. As for Billy, his old friend wouldn't expect him to say much, about the kitten or otherwise. That's why he'd hit Billy up for a ride in the first place. He was in no mood for small talk. And Billy would understand that without being told. All Luke wanted to do was to be quiet and think about Sophia. All he wanted to do was figure out what he was going to *say* to Sophia. So, while Billy kept up both sides of the conversation, Luke stared morosely at each passing mile marker and thought about what he was going to say to his brother's widow.

What in the hell am I going to say to you, Sophia? What the hell *could* he say?

By the time Luke caught a glimpse of Bent Tree over the horizon, he still hadn't thought up a good answer to that question. Maybe there wasn't one.

"This's good." Luke gestured for Billy to pull over at Bent Tree's entrance.

"Are you sure, man? I can take you all the way in." Billy had the good sense not to mention Luke's leg or the cane he had to use to get around.

"This is good." Luke repeated. The slow walk up the long drive would push back his arrival time. Anything to stall the inevitable was okay with him. He had no idea how Sophia was going to react to him. Was she going to hug him or hit him? It was a hard one to gauge. Luke gently picked up the kitten and put him back in the box. The kitten immediately started to cry, but Luke refused to look at him again. He grabbed his cane and pushed the door open. Once his feet were on the ground, he paused for a minute, balanced, and then pulled his sea bag out of the bed of the truck and hoisted it onto his shoulder.

"Thanks, brother. 'ppreciate it." Luke reached across the seat, over the crying kitten, and shook Billy's hand.

"No problem, man. Anything I can do to help," Billy said, and Luke knew he meant it. "And don't be a stranger while you're here. Drop by. Meet the wife and kids."

Luke leaned on his cane for support. "I'll see what I can do. Things are…" His voice trailed off for a moment as he searched for the right word. "Complicated."

For the first time, Billy's grin faded. He looked down at the steering wheel. "You know, we were all real sorry to hear about Danny. I mean… We all knew it could happen. Lots of folks are headin' over to Iraq and not comin' back. But you never expect it to happen to someone you know…." Billy shook his head slowly. "I just didn't expect it to happen to Danny."

"I know. Me, neither." He had seen a lot of death in the past six years, but to lose his brother, his *twin,* was… unbearable. If he was back in action, he could bury the pain and forget it for a while. But here? In Montana, with his grieving family and Daniel's grieving widow? The pain was going to be front and center, in his face, all the time. With a definitive nod, Luke ended the conversation. "Give my best to your family."

"Will do, Luke. Will do. To yours, too." Billy shifted into gear. "And if I don't see you, Merry Christmas, man."

"Merry Christmas." The kitten wouldn't stop crying. Luke shut the door.

Billy saluted and started to pull away. Without thinking about it, and without knowing why he did it, Luke reached out and banged the side of the truck with his cane.

Billy's brakes squeaked; the truck stopped. Luke yanked open the door.

"Dammit, Billy. Give me the damn kitten!"

Sophia Lee Brand was beginning to think that she had made a *huge* mistake. At first she had thought it was a great idea to stay behind while her in-laws went elsewhere for Thanksgiving. She had thought, *foolishly,* that the peace and quiet would do her a world of good. Not to mention that a three-hour car ride while she was eight months pregnant seemed like a slow form of torture. She had to pee *all the time*. So, she had stayed behind. Insisted upon it, in fact. And now she was bored senseless! One week of solitude was more than enough for a Boston girl stuck in the west, thank you kindly. Week two was going to be excruciating! Thank God for her to-do lists!

Sophia leaned over the kitchen counter and perused her latest list. It wasn't even close to supper time and she had already checked off most of the items.

"I really need a longer list!" She stood upright, stretched backward a bit to ease the pressure from the small of her back. She rubbed her hands over her rounded stomach in a circular motion, looked down at her growing abdomen and laughed. "I'm one big belly."

"All right, Danny boy," she said to the baby nestled in her stomach. "There's no time like the present." She moved over to the fridge and started the next project on her list: make a giant salad. She dragged every raw vegetable out of the fridge that she could find, rummaged through drawers and moved bottles and jars out of the way. Once she had located every last veggie, she carefully and methodically sharpened a knife. She took her time. It was only a little after 3:00 p.m. and she had absolutely no idea what she would do with herself until bedtime.

"Let's have a little 'get in the mood' music, shall we?" Sophia read the titles on the CDs stacked at the end of the long counter. "No. No. Really, no. Seriously, no! And…ah…yes. Mr. Van Morrison." She slid the CD into the player and turned up the volume.

She waited for the first notes to play before she turned up the volume even louder. "I can play it as loud as I *want* to. Who's gonna complain way out here in the boonies?" She patted her stomach. "Are you going to complain, my baby? No, you're not, because you're gonna *love* Mr. Morrison just like your daddy did."

On the way back to the veggies, she grabbed a large salad bowl and then got busy chopping and dicing. The music helped get a rhythm going, and before she knew it she was moving on to the pile of carrots. While she worked, she thought of Daniel.

She paused her chopping for a minute, closed her eyes and conjured his face. In her mind's eye, she could easily see his strong, squared jaw, the bright, sky-blue eyes and his trademark smile.

"Hmm. So handsome." This was said with a sigh as she continued with her chopping.

Sophia had a theory, and it had actually helped her cope. She figured that if she thought about Daniel all of the time, she would burn into her brain the little details that made him so incredibly special. She never wanted to run out of things to tell her son about his father. And, of course, she never wanted to forget the little details of Daniel that had always been just for her, like the natural sweet almond scent of his skin and the sensation of his fingers on her neck as he brushed her hair over her shoulder. And his voice. The sound of Daniel's voice always sent a shiver up her spine. Especially the husky way he would say her name when he reached for her in the morning....

"Hello, Sophia."

Sophia was in midchop of a very hardheaded carrot when the sound of her name startled her. She simultaneously spun her head around and pressed the knife down hard. The knife missed the carrot and cut the tip of her finger.

"Ow! Shoot!" Sophia jerked her hand away from the cutting board, but otherwise ignored the wounded finger. Instead, she stared at Luke. He was standing in the kitchen doorway wearing his dress blues and a long gray overcoat; feet planted apart, shoulders squared, sky-blue eyes slightly narrowed. He stood before her proudly in his uniform. Strong. Unyielding. Totally masculine. He looked so much like Daniel that her heart started to thud in her chest, the muscles in her legs gave way, and she had to force herself not to cross the room, throw herself into his arms and squeeze the breath right out of him.

That's not Daniel! That's Luke. Stay put! You and Luke don't hug.

"You're bleeding," Luke said.

"What?"

"Your finger." Luke didn't move from his spot. "It's bleeding."

Sophia looked at her finger. Luke was right. It was indeed bleeding. Quite a bit, actually. The blood had trickled down the length of her pointer finger and was pooling into the palm of her hand; some had gotten smeared on her mother-in-law's counter. Under normal circumstances, she would have quickly fixed the finger, cleaned the counter and gotten back to work. But these weren't normal circumstances, and it appeared that she had temporarily lost control over her body. She couldn't seem to move.

But Luke could. In two long strides he was by her side. She saw him wince whenever he put pressure on his left leg. It was strange to see Luke hurt. He had always seemed so invincible to her. Luke flipped on the cold water and guided her finger beneath the stream. She was still pondering on the warm brand his fingers had left on her skin while he moved down the counter to search a nearby drawer.

"Right corner cabinet, top shelf, all the way in the back." Sophia pointed with her good pointer finger.

"Band-aids?" Luke gave her a quizzical look.

"Your mother's been rearranging since the day we got the news about your leg."

Once Sophia said that, it made perfect sense. Barbara Brand didn't cry when she was upset. She rearranged stuff. Luke located a step stool. "Okay, where are they again?"

"All the way to the right." Sophia waved her hand for him to move farther down. "Top shelf. Behind the olives."

Luke stabbed the off button on the CD player before he forced himself up the steps. He ignored the pain in his leg and concentrated on working his way through the maze his mother had set up between himself and the Band-aids. Luke grabbed the box, threw them onto the counter and got down off the step stool.

Luke put the box of Band-aids on the counter next

to Sophia. "Not exactly the most convenient place to put *first aid* stuff."

That made Sophia laugh. "No. It's not. But none of us were about to argue with your mom. Not your dad, not me. Certainly not Tyler, he's so easygoing."

One side of Luke's upper lip curled into something that vaguely resembled a smile. "I don't blame you." He knew better than to argue with his mother, too. Most people did. He unwrapped a Band-aid. "Here. Give me your finger."

Something clicked on in her brain and she went from foggy to full throttle. She didn't want him to touch her again. The heat from his body, the smell of his skin, made her feel light-headed. He was too much like Daniel. She didn't know how to react to him, and that ticked her off!

She held her finger away from him. "I can do it myself."

Luke gave her a look that she was certain was meant to intimidate her into cooperating. "Sophia. Don't be a pain."

She narrowed her eyes. "I'm not being a pain."

"That would be a first," Luke said under his breath. Then, more loudly, "Just give me your finger."

"Just give me the stupid Band-aid." She held out her hand. His voice, so much like *Daniel's* voice, sent a shiver right up her spine.

Luke grabbed her arm firmly, held her hand in place and put the Band-aid on her finger. "Now, was that so difficult?"

God, Luke irritated her! He always had. He was so *bossy.* Domineering. Why had she thought, for *one minute,* that things would be different between them now?

She grabbed a rag off the kitchen faucet and wiped up the blood from the counter. "Thanks," she said sullenly.

"You're welcome," he replied, with a hint of sarcasm. He wasn't about to climb up on the step stool again. Instead, he tossed the box of Band-aids down the length of the counter.

Silently, she rinsed the rag and wrung it out before she turned back to him. "What are you doing here, anyway? Your parents said you wouldn't be here for another week."

He almost told her the truth, that he had come home early to see her. That he knew his family was away and she was alone. But he didn't. Instead, he said plainly, "Change of plans."

A flash of anger flushed Sophia's cheeks. "Well, I wish you *hadn't* changed your plans. Not if all you intend to do is fight with me the entire time you're here. If you hadn't noticed—" she pulled her sweater tightly over her belly and splayed both hands over her stomach "—I'm a little bit busy here with your nephew, and the last thing I need is to have you hanging around, bullying me."

When she stopped talking, the anger ebbed as quickly as it had risen. The last bit of her energy slipped away with the anger. Suddenly, she felt exhausted. She always felt exhausted now because of the baby, but she did her best to fight it all day long until the fatigue finally won out. Sophia moved over to the table and sat down heavily.

Sophia's words struck him as if she had slapped him in the face. The last thing he *ever* expected Sophia to call him was a bully. He raised an eyebrow at her. "Bullying you?"

He would have joined her at the table, but his leg was

killing him. Instead, he leaned back on the counter and crossed his arms over his chest.

Sophia waved her hand before she rested her chin on it. "All right. Perhaps *bullying* is the wrong word. But you know what I mean. You've always looked for a reason to pick a fight with me. Always. And to tell you the truth, now that Daniel's gone, I thought things might be different. I thought you might actually make an effort to be nice to me. Stop giving me such a hard time all the time."

Next to his mother, Sophia was the only person who could easily cut through his B.S. and make him feel like crap. They were the only two women whose opinion actually mattered to him. And she was right. He was doing exactly what he had promised himself he wouldn't do with her. He had promised himself that he wouldn't fall into the same old pattern with her. He'd stop looking for reasons to fight with her and handle her gently. Things would be different. He would change his ways and get along with Sophia. That's what Daniel would have wanted. That's what he needed to do, for everyone's sake, including his own.

"Okay." Luke's tone was steady and quiet. "We've obviously gotten off on the wrong foot here."

Sophia drew her eyebrows together. "We?"

Luke eyed her, blew out his breath and then started over. "Okay...*I* got off on the wrong foot here. Let me go upstairs, take a shower. We'll try it again later."

Sophia nodded. Seemed like a good idea. The two of them were going to be under the same roof for the next month or so. They were going to have to learn how to get along. She was willing, if he was willing. "I'm in Daniel's room. Your mom fixed up your room for you, of course. We're sharing the bathroom. That a problem for you?"

"No." He took a step forward, but stopped abruptly. A sharp pain ripped through his left thigh.

Sophia saw Luke's tanned face pale as he bent over to put his hand on his leg. She forced herself to stand up. "Should you be walking around so much? Why don't you have a cane?"

Luke straightened upright and took in a deep breath through his nose. He *should* be using his cane, but he had some stupid notion that he didn't want Sophia to see him with it. He hadn't wanted her to think he was weak. Screw it! She was going to see him use it eventually anyway. It might as well be now. It had to be now. "It's in the hall. With my bag."

Sophia went into the hall, grabbed the cane and brought it to Luke. "A whole heck of a lot of good it was doing you over there."

Luke leaned on the cane. He suddenly looked beat. "I don't like the damn thing."

Sophia didn't like Luke's pallor, or the beads of sweat that had popped out along his forehead. Luke had always been so combative with her, but she still cared about him.

"Do you need help?" she asked.

Luke had to stop himself from snapping at her. He measured his words, regulated his tone. "No. I've got it." Offhandedly, he added, "Thanks."

Luke slowly made his way to the hallway. He looked between the narrow stairs and his duffel bag at the entrance. He considered leaving the bag behind. His leg was throbbing. He just wanted to get to his room and get off his feet.

"Luke?" Sophia's voice made him stop.

"Yes?"

"Is your coat meowing?"

Chapter Two

For a moment, Luke stared at Sophia and tried to make sense of her words. Then it hit him. The kitten! "Shit! I mean, shoot!" He was going to have to start watching his mouth in his mother's house. And in front of Sophia. One raised eyebrow in his direction made Luke acutely aware of Sophia's displeasure with his use of profanity in her presence. Luke looked down into his gaping pocket at the sleepy-eyed kitten. "Sorry, little guy. You were so frickin' quiet I forgot all about you."

"What do you have?" Sophia peeked into his pocket. "A kitten? You have a *kitten*? Where'd you get him? Or her?"

Luke leaned his cane against the wall and used both hands to scoop the kitten out of his pocket. "It's a 'he.' Billy suckered me into taking him. That ride from the airport wasn't free."

"Ah, yes. I've heard about Billy and his strays." Sophia moved closer, her face delighted. She loved kittens. So had Daniel. "Hi," she said to the kitten. Then, to Luke, "What's his name?"

Luke examined the kitten, took in his coal-black fur and his giant golden eyes. Black and gold were Ranger colors. "Ranger." The name popped out of his mouth, and it seemed to fit.

"Ranger," Sophia repeated. Daniel had been a ranger in the army. Briefly. "I like it. Daniel would have liked it, too. He loved cats."

Luke put the kitten on his shoulder. "Yes, he did." He supposed that was the real reason he had decided to keep the little guy. It's what Dan would have done.

Luke reached for his cane, accidentally pushed it, and the stupid thing slid down the wall and landed on the ground. Sophia and Luke both eyeballed it. With her hands on her hips, Sophia finally said, "I can get myself down there, but I'm gonna need help getting back up." She patted her bulging belly with a self-effacing smile. "I'm a little top-heavy nowadays."

Luke used one hand to hold the kitten on his chest. "I'll get you back up."

Sophia tilted her head. "Teamwork, then." She carefully lowered herself down onto her haunches and picked up the cane. With her other hand she reached out and clasped Luke's outstretched fingers. Luke braced himself and used the strength of his biceps to bring her up steady and smooth. As he pulled her up, while her eyes were averted, Luke took the opportunity to admire the angles of her beautiful face. How many times had her image kept him company while he was away? He knew her face well. He had memorized every landmark years ago. The slightly upturned tip of her nose, the smattering of freckles across the bridge. The honey tone of her skin that perfectly matched the honey high-lights in her long, straight hair. Her full mouth. She had married his brother, but he had seen her first. Fell in love with her on the spot. Had loved her ever since; secretly and from a distance. Always from a distance.

"Here ya go." Sophia handed the cane over and then scratched the back of Ranger's neck. "Why don't you leave him with me while you take a shower? I could use the company."

Luke had been wondering how the heck he was going to get himself, his bag, and now the kitten all upstairs. Her suggestion sounded like a good one. "What about the whole pregnancy-and-cat thing…"

Sophia waved it off. "Oh, please. We'll just trim his nails so he won't accidentally scratch me and you'll handle all the kitty-box duties. My mom had cats when she was pregnant with me, and I turned out fine. Not to worry…"

"All right." Luke tried to pull Ranger from his shoulder, but the kitten was determined to stay put. Ranger used his claws to cling to Luke's overcoat as if it was Velcro.

"Here, let me help you." Sophia carefully extracted Ranger from Luke's coat. She held him in the crook of her arm and gave Luke the once-over. She moved her finger up and down. "Why do you still have your coat on, anyway? Here, take it off and I'll hang it up. No sense in you taking it upstairs."

Luke shrugged out of the overcoat, glad to have it off, and handed it to Sophia. She nodded her approval and hung it up on the coat rack by the door.

"One more thing," Luke said with a gruff tone. He checked himself and adjusted his tone. "If you don't mind."

"Hmm?"

"Drag my bag over here for me, will ya? I'll get it on my shoulder from here. I don't want you lifting it. It's too heavy."

"No prob." Sophia dragged the bag over to Luke. She smiled up at him. "Teamwork!" That smile of hers was rarely aimed his way. It caught him off guard, made his stomach clench in response. Without a word, he bent over at the waist and lifted the bag up with a grunt. Once he hooked it onto his shoulder, he headed up the stairs.

"Take your time," Sophia called after him. "I'll just close the door to the kitchen so he has to stay in there with me. We'll see you when you come down."

Luke awakened from his nap, groggy and disoriented. At first he didn't know exactly where he was; it took him a minute to figure it out. He had no idea how long he had slept. All he knew is that it had been light outside when his head hit the pillow and now it was dark. He reached over and fumbled for the lamp on the bedside table. Then he squinted at his watch. It was still on Afghan time. His fuzzy brain calculated the time difference and figured it was closing in on 9:00 p.m.

He couldn't believe he had slept so long. Nearly six hours. He had popped a couple of pain pills before he crashed on the bed. Those pills must have done the trick; he usually could sleep for only an hour or two at a time.

Luke hung his legs off the side of the bed for a moment before he slid off the mattress. He stripped off the rest of his clothes, undressed his wound and headed for the shower. He examined the antique claw-foot tub, with unreasonably high sides, and worked out the most practical way to get himself in it. Once in the shower, he pressed his hands against the back of the wall and let the steaming water run down his back. The water stung as it hit the wound, but it was a good pain.

As the water pummeled his skin, Luke's mind drifted, as it often did, to Sophia. She had surprised him. Honestly, he had expected to find a sniffling, hormonal, wretched woman who spent her waking moments blaming him for Dan's death. He blamed himself, after all, so why shouldn't she? If he hadn't chosen a military life, perhaps Dan wouldn't have joined the army out of the blue. And if he hadn't joined, he'd still be alive today.

He'd thought for sure that Sophia would blame him. He had counted on it. Planned for it. But she didn't seem to. And she certainly wasn't wallowing and weeping. That was a major relief. There were a lot of things that Luke knew how to do. If he had to jump out of a plane to get the job done, he could do it. If something needed to be blown up, not a problem. But comfort a hysterical female? Not his area of expertise.

Luckily for him, Sophia had her act together. He should have known she would. He had no idea what possessed him to doubt her in the first place. Sophia had always been headstrong, determined and upbeat. In the ten years he had known her, he'd never once seen her let life get her down. It was one of the things he had always loved about her. So had Dan, for that matter. Dan and he had disagreed since they were kids, about everything, all of the time. But they had always agreed about the merits of Sophia.

Out of the shower now, Luke dressed the wound, pulled on jeans and a white undershirt. He was starved.

He headed downstairs to raid the fridge and see how Sophia and Ranger were getting on.

Sophia was sitting at the table, writing. Ranger was sitting on the table next to her pad of paper, legs tucked up beneath him, eyes closed. He opened his eyes when he heard the kitchen door open, stood up, stretched into a back arch and then sat down on his haunches.

"Mom would have a fit about that," Luke said. Sophia knew he meant Ranger sitting on the table.

Sophia wrinkled up her nose. "I know." She sighed, heavily. "I know. But to tell you the truth, I was so impressed with his determination to get up here, I didn't have the heart to tell him no."

Luke remembered Ranger's valiant escape from the box. He had felt the same way. "He has that effect." Luke moved to the table and reached out to stroke Ranger's fur. The minute he touched the little guy, he started to purr.

"How's your finger?"

Sophia held up her bandaged finger. "Still attached. How's your leg?"

Luke shot her a wry expression. "Still attached."

Sophia smiled at him, which made the dimple on her left cheek appear.

"What are you doing?" Luke asked. He picked Ranger up and held him next to his heart.

"Making a list of things to do tomorrow. I swear, these lists are the only thing that's kept me sane while your family is at your uncle's for Thanksgiving. He's in pretty bad shape after that surgery he just had. Did you know about that?"

Luke took a seat at the table. He nodded yes.

Sophia clicked the pen so the tip came in and out.

"You know, you should really call your folks and let them know you're here."

"I'll let it be a surprise."

"Okay," Sophia replied, skeptically. "If you say so. But you know how your mom is…."

"She'll be fine."

Sophia made a noise and went back to her list. After a minute, she slapped the pen down on the paper. "Wow. My brain is really fried. You haven't eaten." She pushed herself up. "You've gotta be famished."

"I am."

Sophia opened the refrigerator. She twisted to the side and looked at him. "Chicken and stuffing okay? I made myself a little impromptu Thanksgiving dinner yesterday. Happy belated Thanksgiving, by the way. It's a bummer you had to spend your holiday traveling." She paused to take a breath and then continued. "So? Chicken and stuffing okay?"

"That's fine," Luke said. You always had to wait for Sophia to come up for air before you spoke. "I can fend for myself, you know. I don't want you overdoing it on my account. You're…you know."

She pulled out some Tupperware. "Pregnant? I know. Kind of obvious. But it's not like I'm disabled or an invalid."

Luke's shoulders stiffened. "Neither am I."

Ah yes. The infamous Brand family pride. She knew it well. She found it as equally annoying in Luke as she had in Daniel. "You'd think you wouldn't be so cranky after such a long nap." Of course, the Brand men were well-known for being impossible to get along with if they were hungry. Sophia stopped what she was doing and leaned back on the counter. "I wasn't calling you an invalid, but the truth is the truth. Your leg is screwed up. Mine isn't. So, do you want me to help you out or not?"

The expression on Luke's face undoubtedly sent his military underlings running for cover. She knew him well enough not to be impressed. "Yes? No? What shall it be, Captain?"

"Do you always have to be so dramatic over every little thing?" Luke answered a question with a question; another Brand family trait.

"I'll take that as a yes." She popped the lids off the containers and piled food high on a plate.

While Sophia prepared his meal, Luke couldn't take his eyes off her. Thoughts of her had been his constant companion, but this was the first time he'd ever been alone with her. This was the first time he'd ever had her all to himself. The circumstances weren't ideal, but having Sophia with him now felt as if the planets had aligned for him. And he was enjoying just sitting back and watching her.

"How are you feeling?" he asked her.

Sophia's ponytail swung to the side as she spun her head around to look at him over her shoulder. "Honestly, I've had a great pregnancy…all things considered. I've been exercising, of course, staying active. I have a friend who's a personal trainer and she helps me choose the right foods, pick safe exercises. I haven't even been all that tired, until recently." She shrugged one shoulder. "The worst of it is missing Daniel, wanting him to be here with me. He always used to say that he couldn't wait to see me pregnant." Sophia paused for a minute to compose herself. At times, the emotions would well up without warning and she would have to push back the tears. "I suppose we shouldn't have waited so long to have a family. We were waiting until he finished school and my practice was more stable." Lower, almost under her breath, she added, "Stupid."

"You couldn't have seen this coming, Soph. None of us plan for this sort of thing. No one would get out of bed, if we did," Luke said in a low, even tone. "But you're right about one thing, though. He always wanted to see you pregnant. He always thought you'd make a great-looking pregnant woman." His eyes swept her body unbeknownst to her. "He was right."

"Thanks," Sophia said with a small smile. The timer dinged and Sophia pulled the plate out of the microwave. "Of course, my face is puffy, my ankles are swollen and I have to urinate *constantly*." She put the plate down in front of him and smiled. "TMI, right?"

Luke shook his head; as she set the plate down, he noticed the simple gold wedding band that still encircled her left ring finger. He wasn't surprised that she still wore her wedding band; she had always been loyal to Dan. In life, and now in death.

The minute she moved her hand away, he hunched over his plate and started to dig in.

"Something to drink?"

Luke chewed fast, and then swallowed hard before he spoke. "Water's good."

She brought a glass of water back to the table with her and then sat down beside him. Ranger had found his way back to the food Sophia had scrounged up for him. The Brand family had taken in so many strays over the years that it was standard operating procedure to have emergency pet supplies on hand.

"The moral of this story is, I feel pretty good and I have to stay active in order to maintain a modicum of sanity out here in the boonies. So, I don't mind helping you out while you rest your leg a bit…if you can put your male pride aside for a second or two."

Luke wasn't really paying attention to what she was saying; he was shoveling in his food as if he hadn't eaten for days. He ate like a man who was used to being surrounded by other men vying for the same food. He protected his food with one arm, leaned forward and got the food to his mouth as quickly as possible.

"Luke," she asked with surprise, "what happened to your table manners?"

Luke paused from his shoveling for a second, sat up and moved his arms off the table. He glanced up at her. "Better?"

"Much." She shook her head at him. "I take it you like the food? Or, were you just that hungry?"

Luke gulped the water down before he said, "It was pretty damn good."

Sophia picked up the plate and rinsed it in the sink. "Glad you liked it." When she returned to her spot at the table, Luke had Ranger in his lap.

"Find any clippers when you found the cat food?" Luke was examining the kitten's claws.

"Yes. Finally. I wish your mom would find a different outlet when she's upset. None of us can ever find anything when she's done." Sophia chuckled and shook her head. "I put them over there on the counter." She made to get up again. Luke's warm hand on her arm stopped her.

"You sit. I'll get them."

She decided to let him win this one and didn't protest. He returned with the clippers and the kitten. Once seated, he flipped Ranger over on his back and put him down gently on his lap.

"You've done this before."

"Yes, I have," Luke replied. His mom's soft spot for animals was well-known in the community; everyone knew where to drop off the strays.

Ranger was crying and squirming on Luke's lap. "If you steady his hind legs, we'll get this done quickly."

She scooted her chair closer and reached out to stop Ranger from kicking his legs, while Luke started to trim his front claws. She was so close to him that the fresh scent of his skin invaded her senses. He smelled just like Daniel when he was straight out of the shower: almonds mixed with the scent of soap. She couldn't stop herself from taking his scent deeply into her lungs. Her long intake of breath caught Luke's attention. He looked up from his task, caught her eye and said, "Teamwork."

Nothing in his face read humor, but she saw a glint of mirth that lurked behind the intense depth of his light blue eyes. She leaned back a bit and resisted the urge to bury her nose in his neck. That's what she used to do with Daniel. It used to be one of her favorite things to do.

"There you go, little man. All done." Luke easily turned the kitten upright and let him down on the ground. Ranger hopped forward a couple of steps before he stopped and licked his shoulder to release some of his irritation.

Sophia watched Ranger, glad for the distraction that pulled attention away from the way Luke's nearness made her heart race. "I was actually starting to think that you were going to sleep through the night."

"I'm surprised I got any shut-eye at all, to tell you the truth." Luke leaned back in the chair and stretched out his left leg. He rubbed his hands across his cropped hair. Daniel had always worn his light brown hair shaggy and long. Sophia couldn't remember the last time she had seen Luke without what she termed "Marine hair." Looking at him now, she was reminded of the first time she had seen Daniel after he had enlisted in the army; he had looked just like Luke in that moment. When they had made love, conceived the child she was carrying, for a split second, she had thought of Luke.

"What?" Luke asked her, an eyebrow raised in question. She must have been giving him an odd look.

"Just thinking."

"Anything interesting?"

"No."

Just remembering that I had thought of you when Daniel and I conceived this child...

Luke was growing a goatee; there was a faint outline of stubble that encircled his mouth. Her fingers had the strangest urge to reach out and follow the goatee trail around his lips, of all the stupid things!

"I think we should put Ranger in the hall bathroom upstairs. What do you think?"

"What?" She hadn't been paying attention to the conversation; she had been distracted by his lips.

"The hall bathroom. Ranger. The kitty box. What do you think?"

"Oh. Yeah. Makes sense." Those words were followed by a wide yawn. "I think it's time for me to start thinking about bed. It's been a long day."

It took several slow trips, but between the two of them, they managed to get Ranger, his food and the kitty box upstairs into the hall bathroom. Sophia molded a bed out of towels and turned on a low nightlight before she shut the door. Ranger was hooked up.

Luke and Sophia faced each other outside of their respective bedroom doors. There was an awkward moment of silence before they both finally said good-night.

Once inside their rooms, they ran back into each other on their sides of the adjoining bathroom.

Luke held on to his door. "Ladies first."

Sophia agreed. She stepped into the bathroom. She added, "Make sure you knock, mister. Let's not have any unfortunate moments."

He knew what she was getting at. She didn't want him to accidentally walk in on her while she was naked in the head.

"Understood," he said before he closed the door firmly shut. He heard the lock click, and that made him smile a bit.

Fifteen minutes later, she knocked on his door. "Okay. Your turn."

He got himself in and out of the bathroom as fast as possible. He popped a couple of painkillers into his mouth and then waited impatiently for them to knock him out. He tossed and turned; he tried to find a comfortable way to position his leg, but he never found it. Instead, he lay on his back with his hands folded behind his head, and imagined Sophia in her bed. It took all of his willpower not to cross to her room and pull her into his arms.

God, he loved her.

God, he wanted her.

But she loved Dan. In her eyes, he would always be second best to his twin. He knew that. Had always known it. Now, he would just have to continue to live with it.

Sophia wasn't having any better luck sleeping than Luke. It was almost impossible to find a comfortable position to sleep at this stage of the pregnancy game. She had three pillows jammed along her back for support, and one pillow jammed between her legs to keep her knees from digging into each other. Little Danny had decided, for some unknown reason, to change his position the minute she lay down to go to sleep. He had seemed perfectly content in his original position the entire night, but once she closed her eyes, he stuffed his feet up under her rib cage and started to spin around. It felt as if he was trying to make a break for it!

So, when Ranger started crying at the top of his lungs, she was awake to hear it. She sighed heavily and rolled herself out of bed. The wood floor was cold on her bare feet as she quietly made her way to the door. She opened the door, stepped outside of her room and bumped right into a nearly naked Luke. The only thing the man had on was tight white boxer briefs. She hoped that her expression didn't change as her eyes flitted up and down the length of him.

The frame was the same as Daniel's, yes. But this build was all Luke. His body was lean and muscular from years of fighting and surviving. Her eyes settled on the bandage that encircled Luke's sculpted thigh before she swung them back up to Luke's face. At that moment, she was genuinely grateful for the dim light in the hall. She had no doubt that her face was stained bright red with a blush.

"I'll get him," Luke said. "You go back to bed."

"Are you sure?"

"Yeah. I got it."

Sophia removed herself quickly back to her room. The racing of her heart, she suspected, had absolutely nothing to do with her husband and everything to do with Luke. And she hated it. What kind of woman would bury her husband, carry his child and then respond physically to another man?

"A seriously disturbed one," Sophia scolded herself

as she pounded the pillows behind her, squeezed her eyes shut and willed herself to fall asleep.

Luke was having his own issues. Ranger was curled up in a ball next to his ear on the pillow, happily purring his fool head off. Luke, on the other hand, was wide awake and fully aroused. Seeing Sophia in her nightgown, her long silky hair spilling over her shoulders and onto her breasts, made blood flow rapidly into parts of his body that had no business waking up. But she had just looked so damned sexy in her modest cotton nightgown with the light from the stairs revealing the outline of her shapely legs. Even the bulge of her pregnant belly was a turn-on.

"God… You're sick, man," Luke said to himself. He balled his hands into a fist and waited for the arousal to ebb. He had no business horn-dogging after Sophia. No business at all! Luke felt like hitting something, so he pounded the mattress with his fists. Why hadn't the pills kicked in? Only sleep would annihilate the vulnerable, sensual image of Sophia fresh out of bed that was now scorched into his brain. Sleep couldn't get here soon enough. Not by a long shot.

Chapter Three

Luke woke up the next morning feeling hungover from the meds. He had managed to sleep off and on, but for the most part, he had tossed and turned all night. He couldn't get his leg comfortable and he couldn't get Sophia out of his mind. Being so close to her, without Dan as a buffer, was not something he had been prepared to handle. She made him feel *out of control*. He didn't like it.

"Square yourself away, marine. Real quick," Luke said to his reflection before he flipped open the hinged bathroom mirror and looked for a razor in the medicine cabinet. He knew he'd find one; his mom was always prepared. What he wasn't expecting to find was a neatly organized row of Sophia's favorite fragrances.

The first time he had ever laid eyes on Sophia, she was working behind a fragrance counter in a local department store. She had been talking with a customer, a perfume bottle loosely held in her hand. Her hair was swept up into a haphazard twist and her lovely face was completely devoid of makeup. The sight of her throwing her head back as she laughed stopped him in his tracks. She laughed without reservation; her positive energy sucked him in. He couldn't seem to take his eyes off her. In an instant, he was crazy, head over heels for her, and he had been ever since.

Luke glanced over at the adjoining bathroom door that led to Sophia's bedroom. He had heard her moving around a couple of hours ago, so he knew she was already downstairs. He reached over and checked to make sure the door was locked before he pulled the first fragrance bottle down.

"Stalker," Luke said quietly to himself with a self-effacing half smile. He popped the top off the first bottle and brought it up to his nose. The minute the perfume reached his senses, he thought "Sophia." To Luke, Sophia always smelled like something he wanted to eat. She never wore the same fragrance two days in a row, but she did have a lineup of favorites, and Luke recognized them all.

One by one, Luke spent a moment with each of Sophia's fragrances. Each one conjured up a memory of Sophia. From Luke's vantage point, Dan had won the ultimate prize the day he married her. Luke snapped the top onto the last bottle and got back to the business of shaving the stubble off his face. He moved his head side to side and checked out the goatee that was taking shape. A couple of days more and it might actually look like something. He wondered if Sophia would like him with it. The minute that thought crossed his mind, he gripped each side of the sink, dropped his head and shook it.

Unacceptable, Brand!

The sooner he got back to his life in the corps, the better off he'd be. He didn't make sense in civilian clothes. He sure as hell didn't make sense when he was around Sophia; he needed to figure out a way to shove his feelings back into place. He had been doing it for years; it should be second nature. But it wasn't. Keeping his heart closed to Sophia was like trying to stop his lungs from wanting to take in air. Whenever she was near him, he had an overwhelming urge to hold her face in his hands, look into those sweet hazel-green eyes and tell her that he loved her. That he had always loved her. Which would, of course, be the worst mistake of his life. His confession would freak Sophia out, and any plans he had to play a big role in his nephew's life would get eighty-sixed. He couldn't risk that happening. He just couldn't risk it.

Luke stared down his own image in the mirror. "Maintain your military bearing, marine. That's all you have to do. Maintain your military bearing."

Luke pushed himself away from the sink and headed downstairs. Sophia smiled at him in greeting. She was on the phone; she mouthed the name "Tyler" and raised her eyebrows at him. He shook his head. There were five kids in the Brand clan, including him. Tyler was the middle child; he was sandwiched between two sets of twins; Dan and Luke were the oldest, and Jordan and Josephine were the youngest. Out of the three boys and two girls, Tyler had turned out to be the only true rancher in the bunch. He took after their dad, from his tall, lanky build to his love for the land. Luke was proud of him, looked forward to seeing him, but he wasn't ready for a reunion just yet. His entire focus was on Sophia. The rest of the family had to take a backseat.

"Okay." Sophia said into the phone after a pause. "Thanks for checking up on me. Tell your mom and dad that I'm fine. Danny and I are doing just fine." She rested her hand on her stomach as she spoke those words. "Okay. I'm glad your uncle's feeling better. And listen, have some fun while you're there. Stop worrying about me. I'll see you when you guys get back. All right. Bye, Tyler."

Sophia hung up the phone. "You could have at least told *Tyler* you're here. He's as tight-lipped as you are."

"And ruin the surprise?"

Luke said this with a deadpan expression. She could rarely read him, and this time was no different, but something in her gut told her that Luke's early arrival didn't have much to do with surprising his family. She just couldn't figure out what else it could be.

She put the kettle on for tea. "I already got the third degree from my parents this morning…again. They want me to have this baby in Boston. I can't really blame them, this is their first grandchild. But this is your parents' first grandchild, too. And I don't know…I think it's more important for your parents because this is Daniel's son."

"No matter what you do, someone's always gonna be ticked off." Luke shrugged. "Do what's best for you, make yourself happy; everyone else will fall in formation. Or not."

Sophia smiled faintly. "You're right. Not always easy to do, though. For me, anyway. Coffee?"

Luke nodded. She brought him a cup of black coffee. He was surprised she remembered that he didn't take cream and sugar.

"Eggs okay?"

"I wish you'd stop waiting on me."

"I wish you'd stop giving me a hard time about something I want to do. You're actually doing me a favor. My days are packed in Boston with clients and meetings, friends, shopping. I'm used to being on my BlackBerry all of the time at home. I swear I'm having serious withdrawal because the reception is so bad here. I actually have to stand up on the window seat in my room and smash myself up against the wall in order to get just one lousy bar! I *have* to find stuff to do here, or I swear to you I'll go stark raving mad." She pulled eggs out of the fridge and located a pan. "I mean, your family's great. Your mom, your dad, Tyler…all of them. They've been wonderful to me. But I'm a city girl. I'm used to keeping up the pace all day long. Coming and going as I please. Out here, I feel like I'm stuck in slow motion." She paused from her task for a minute so she could punctuate her words with her hands. "Quite frankly, it's driving me nuts. There are only so many sunsets I can admire, so much foliage I can appreciate. I never thought I'd hear myself say this, but bring on the traffic and the noise." She dug in the cabinet for a bag of decaffeinated green tea. "And I can only hope that your parents aren't going to want me to make this a permanent situation once Danny is born."

Luke nodded. His mom just might try to convince Sophia to stay. His mom was all about family, and she would want to see Dan's son grow. "It's gotta be tough to be away from your business. Who's taking care of your clients while you're away?" Luke asked, before he took a sip of coffee.

Sophia started to scramble the eggs, just how he liked them. Another thing she had remembered about him. Dan only ate his fried.

"It's the hardest thing I've ever done, leaving the

business. I've had horrible abandonment issues. What kind of therapist abandons her patients? Luckily I have a great group of therapists in our office who were willing to take on my patients. I still feel bad, though. Like I'm letting them down. Especially during the holidays. I'm booked between Thanksgiving and New Year's. A lot of depression." Sophia took the kettle off the stove and poured the piping-hot water over the tea bag.

"Dealing with your family can do that to a person." Luke nodded.

"The holidays are a tough time. People get depressed if they have to spend time with family, and then other people get depressed if they don't *have* family to make them miserable during the holidays. Either way, the holidays are a therapist's busy season. Kind of like tax season for CPAs." Sophia put the finished eggs on a plate and brought them to Luke. "Here ya go."

"Tax time's probably busy for you, too."

That made Sophia smile. Lately, Luke had been having that effect on her. She liked it. "Come to think of it, I do get a boost during April."

When Sophia leaned over to set the plate on the table, her arm brushed against Luke's. The sensation of his skin against hers set off an instantaneous chain reaction; the fine hairs on her arm stood straight up on end, and wherever his skin had touched hers a trail of goose bumps popped up. Horrified, she immediately started to rub her arm to smooth the goose bumps away.

Luke admired the food on his plate. "This looks really good. Thanks."

"My pleasure." She turned away from him. "Hey… Where's Ranger?"

"I put him in the bathroom. He needs to use the

head," he said, then corrected himself. "I mean the *facilities*."

"Gotcha." Sophia smiled; she continued to rub her arm.

Luke noticed the rubbing, of course. Had to comment, *of course*. "You cold? I'll get a fire started if you want."

Sophia looked down at her arm. She wasn't cold, but what was she going to say, "The feel of your skin on mine gave me goose bumps, Luke"? Not likely! Instead she said, "I'd like that. Tyler or your dad would always build me a fire. I've missed them. Do you need anything else? Toast? Orange juice?"

"I'm good. Thanks."

"Then I'm gonna check on Ranger. Maybe he'll be brave enough to explore downstairs today." That little kitten had been a great distraction. She needed a reason to get away from Luke and the bizarre, completely unacceptable feelings he kicked up inside of her; Ranger was a perfect excuse. This reaction she was having to Luke was starting to get really old. She was obviously having some sort of emotional transference brought on by the fact that Luke looked exactly, for the most part, like Daniel. And it was obvious that she missed Daniel and was transferring some of her unrequited desire on to his twin! It had to be that. She didn't want Luke.

"No. Of course you don't," she said under her breath as she climbed the stairs.

Luke had always been a pain. He had always given her a hard time. He was *nothing* like Daniel, except for the outside package. And even that wasn't exactly the same. Case in point: a nearly naked Luke had looked quite a bit different than a nearly naked Daniel. Okay, perhaps that wasn't the best example she could have thought of. But still!

Sophia reached the top of the stairs and put her hands on her hips as if she were scolding a small child. "You want him to *be* Daniel. But he's not Daniel. He never will be Daniel, so you really need to get a grip, Sophia!" Her psychology degrees were starting to come in handy; she could psychoanalyze herself.

Sophia opened the bathroom door, and Ranger was more than ready to be let out. He dashed out with a trill, wound his way around her ankles and rubbed his head against her leg.

"Hi, buddy." Before Sophia could reach down over her belly to pet him, Ranger voiced another excited trill, stuck his tail straight up in the air and zoomed down the stairs without a moment of hesitation.

She stared after him for a moment, bemused. "He's going to be an absolute terror."

He'd probably do the family a lot of good during the holidays. This would be the first Christmas without Daniel. Perhaps having a crazy kitten in the mix would distract them all.

Before she went back downstairs, Sophia stopped off at the medicine cabinet to pick out the day's fragrance. Unfortunately, none of the self-talk up the stairs stopped her from wondering which fragrance Luke would like.

Irritated, she reached for Daniel's favorite, sprayed it on and went downstairs with a renewed determination not to have any bizarre reactions to Luke.

She found Luke standing in front of the giant bay window that overlooked the ranch. He was staring out at the horizon and seemed to be lost in thought.

"Mission accomplished with the kitty box. Did he come through here?"

"Yeah." One side of his mouth lifted. Sophia could tell by that one small gesture that the kitten cracked Luke up. "He went tearing through here, ran headfirst into the cabinets, shook it off like nothing happened, jumped up a foot in the air, spun around and went flying back toward the library."

"That kitten is a menace. Your dad is going to hit the roof when he sees him." Sophia laughed. She picked up her tea and walked over to stand next to Luke. Perhaps she stood closer to him than she should have, but once she was there, she didn't have any desire to be anywhere else.

"At first. But he's always the one who gets attached the quickest," Luke said as he continued to stare at the horizon.

"It must feel good to be home, especially with all of this," she said of the snowcapped mountains in the distance. "It's getting a bit old for me, but this is your home."

Again, Luke was quiet, as he often was. He stood stock-still, but Sophia could feel his body become tense beside her. She almost moved away, worried she was invading his space, but something made her stay put.

All Luke could do was keep his eyes trained forward. He wanted nothing more than to drape his arm around Sophia's shoulders and pull her close until her body was molded into his. She was wearing his favorite fragrance. She smelled like citrus and freshly cut grass, and he wanted to bury his face in her neck and breathe her in.

And then she would slap me.

Luke shook his head at himself before he drained his cup.

"What?" Sophia noticed him shaking his head.

"Nothing. I think it's time for a fire."

There was something raw in his voice that quickened her pulse. She nodded her head and put some distance between herself and Luke. "I'm going to check my email real quick and then I'll be back down."

They both went their separate ways, headed in two completely different directions. No matter how hard Sophia tried, she couldn't stop her body from reacting to Luke. And it seemed that little Danny was having his own reaction to his uncle's voice. Was it her imagination, or did her baby seem to get more active whenever Luke was around?

Being around Luke was tying her up in knots on the inside. She felt like an absolute lunatic. She was hormonal and grieving, away from her friends and family, and now she was faced with her husband's twin. No wonder she was confused. But she had to make sense of it all and do it quickly. After all, Luke had never liked her, not from the very first day that Daniel had introduced them to each other. If he had even a remote clue what was in her head, he'd dislike her even more. This tentative truce he had forged with her for Daniel's sake would be ruined.

She smoothed her hand over her stomach. "We're not going to let that happen, are we, Danny boy? No. We're not."

More than anything, she wanted Luke to be a big part of her son's life. She couldn't screw it up. She wouldn't *let* herself screw it up. Instead of booting up her laptop, Sophia did something she rarely allowed herself to do; she curled up on the bed, buried her face into a pillow and cried.

After she cried, she slept. And both activities seemed to do her a world of good. When she awakened an hour later she felt a million times better, and she went downstairs with a renewed sense of purpose. It wasn't like her to let things eat at her. She liked to bring things out in the open; clear the air. That was just the way she was; that was the therapist in her. And, even though Luke wasn't exactly the most approachable guy in the world, she wanted to believe that his bark was really much more serious than his bite. She was just going to have to tell him how she was feeling, and he was just going to have to listen. Like it or not.

Sophia found Luke in the library. The fire had died down and the library felt to her as if she was slipping into a warm bath. It was the perfect temperature. Luke was sitting on one end of an overstuffed couch, head back, eyes shut. Ranger was perched on the armrest beside him. When Ranger saw her, he trilled but didn't move.

"Nice fire," she said.

"Hmm." That was the extent of Luke's reply.

Sophia sat down at the other end of the couch. She sank deep into the cushions and realized that she wasn't getting back up unless Luke agreed to pull her out. Sophia slid her butt forward and leaned back. She rested her hands on her belly.

"My friends tell me it's perfectly normal to get tired of being pregnant." She sighed. "I look like I swallowed a basketball, but at least I have a comfortable place to rest my hands." She smiled at herself after she said that.

"Hmm."

"Are you even listening to me?"

Luke cracked an eye open. "No."

Sophia grabbed a pillow and smacked him in the head with it. "Thanks a lot, Luke. That's really sensitive!"

She saw his chest moving; saw the corner of his upper lip lift. The man was actually chuckling. Amazing. Rare. She hit him again.

Luke glanced over at her. "When has anyone ever accused me of being sensitive?"

Sophia raised an eyebrow at him. "Good point."

After a minute, exasperated, she said. "Luke! Aren't you going to say 'you don't look like you swallowed a basketball'?"

Luke pushed himself up so suddenly that it caught her off guard. He leaned forward and turned his head toward her. He had a hard, exasperated look on his face. "You don't look like you swallowed a basketball, Sophia," Luke said in a clipped manner; his hand sliced the air as he spoke. "And, honestly, I don't like to hear you say sh…stuff like that about yourself. You're a beautiful woman who looks better eight months pregnant than most women I know who *aren't* pregnant. If you need to put yourself down, don't do it around me anymore."

Sophia was taken aback by Luke's words. Shocked, actually. Just when she thought he was a total jerk, Luke would throw her a curve ball and prove her wrong.

She saluted him. "Aye, aye, el Capitan."

Luke shook his head slightly at her sarcasm before he leaned back into the couch once again. "Can we enjoy the fire now?"

Sophia didn't agree because she had an agenda, but Luke didn't seem to require her consent. He closed his eyes and sighed deeply.

She wasn't completely heartless; she would give him a few moments of quiet before she approached him about the main issue on her mind. He seemed to be in a pretty good mood; no time like the present was a personal motto.

After a couple minutes, Sophia pushed herself up into a more upright position and turned her body so she could look at Luke's profile.

"Luke?"

"Hmm."

"There's something I want to talk to you about."

It took several long seconds for Luke to respond. No doubt he didn't like the phrase, "I have something to talk to you about."

"This isn't what I meant by 'enjoying the fire.'"

"It's important to me." She tapped her finger to her chest, not deterred by the abrasive tone of his voice.

With a sigh, Luke rubbed his hands over his face several times. "What's on your mind?"

Sophia had been mulling over in her mind how she should bring up the subject. There didn't really seem to be any diplomatic way to broach it. Honestly, the direct approach seemed to be her only real option. Besides, Luke was a more "in your face" kind of guy. He was a marine. He'd probably appreciate her not beating around the bush.

"Well, it's like this." She held out her hand. "And I really hope you don't take offense, Luke, because I'm not trying to hurt your feelings…"

"Before I'm ninety, Soph."

"Quit rushing me!" she replied, "I want to make sure that when I've said what I have to say that you're not going to feel bad…."

"Sophia…"

"*Fine*. Here goes." Sophia paused, took in a deep breath, then let the deep breath out, before she said, "Luke… I don't want you to take this the wrong way, but your face really bothers me."

Chapter Four

After the words popped out of her mouth, Sophia felt immediately relieved. Unloaded. It felt really good to get that off her chest.

There, she thought proudly. *It's good for relationship growth to get things out in the open.*

She had absolutely no doubt that this would be good for both of them. They would have an open and honest dialogue about their feelings; about Daniel. About being together without him. Of course, she had never had a serious discussion with Luke before, but after all, Luke and Daniel were twins, right? There had to be *some* similarities in the way they resolved problems.

Daniel was great when it came to hashing things out. And he always had something relevant to say that let her know that he'd really listened to her and that he'd thought about his answer. He never dismissed her. It was one of the many things that she had truly admired about her husband.

Just like Daniel, Luke was taking his time before he responded. He hadn't moved; his eyes were still closed, his head was still resting on the cushion. No doubt he was trying to think of the perfect thing to say....

Sophia sank back into the couch, rested her head in her hand and, for the first time she could remember, she really *looked* at Luke. Her eyes roamed his profile and naturally took an inventory of all of the little Daniel details she loved.

Those were Daniel's ears. One of her favorites spots to nibble on when they made love. So sensitive. It made her wonder, irrationally, if Luke's ears were sensitive, too.

Silly thought.

Of course, the dent in the middle of Luke's nose, which made him look like a prizefighter, didn't mirror Daniel's nose. Daniel's nose had been unaltered from the original design.

By the time her eyes landed on the faint, long scar that ran the length of Luke's jawline, it hit her that Luke was taking an excessive amount of time to respond to her statement.

Sophia opened her mouth to say his name, but clamped it back shut when she heard Luke take in a deep breath through his nose that sounded suspiciously like a snore.

Sophia reached over and poked him in the arm with her finger. "Luke!"

"Hmm?"

"Did you just fall asleep?"

After a long pause. "No."

"Yes, you did!"

"Are you sure?"

"Yes!" she snapped. Typical Luke behavior! Once again, she had given him more credit than he deserved. She had opened her heart, revealed something very personal to her, and he was *snoring!*

She would have thought at this point the man would have the decency to open his eyes. He didn't. Luke didn't move, but Ranger did. The kitten used his back leg to scratch an itch underneath his chin before he moved over to sit on Luke's chest. Ranger plopped down and curled up into a tight ball. Luke didn't bother to move.

"Luke!" she said forcefully.

"What?" Now *he* sounded irritated.

"You fell asleep!"

After a few ticks of the grandfather clock and a few loud Ranger purrs, Luke cracked an eye open and looked at her. "Then, why'd you wake me up?"

Her mouth dropped open. "Are you *serious?*"

"You bet."

He used that abrasive tone that always rubbed her the wrong way, and she felt her blood pressure soar. She wasn't here to play naughty "recruit" to his bad boy "drill sergeant"! She felt like punching him and she wished, at the moment, that she had a violent streak.

Was this some sort of bizarre pregnancy rage, or was Luke just that infuriating to her?

"Luke." Her tone was snappy and she didn't try to curb it. "We were in the middle of a conversation."

Luke stretched, yawned and then stretched again. Finally, his eyes were open. He turned his full attention to Sophia, examined her through heavy-lidded eyes.

"We were?"

Sophia lifted up both her hands and splayed out her

fingers. "Yes! We were! I said that your face bothered me." When she repeated the phrase out loud, it sounded comical to her own ears, but she didn't laugh as she continued. "Didn't you hear me?"

"I heard you." He had the audacity to sound irritated with her. She wasn't the one who had fallen asleep in the middle of an important conversation.

She found herself glaring at him. "And?"

"And *what?*"

"And… What do you have to say about it?"

Luke rubbed his hands over his face, sighed heavily and finally turned his intense gaze back to her. "What do you want me to say? Oh, wait… How 'bout this. You're the therapist. Why don't you tell me what I should have said, since you obviously have my response all planned out for me."

"No." Her words were clipped and articulated with precision. "I didn't have your response planned out for you, thank you kindly. I was waiting for you to add something constructive to the conversation. A temporary lapse of reason, quite obviously!"

"That was a conversation?"

"Luke! Now you're just being thickheaded! Do you have anything to say or not?"

"No."

"Nothing at all?" Her tone was incredulous; her eyebrows were lifted in disbelief. She told the man that his face bothered her and he had nothing to say?

"What's your problem?" she demanded.

Finally, Luke was paying full attention to her. He held on to Ranger as he sat upright. The features of his handsome face hardened; his lips were downturned into a frown. His eyes were dark and unreadable.

"I'm not the one with the problem." His tone was

sharp, controlled. Slightly mocking. "Your face doesn't bother me all that much."

Sophia was silent; her mind raced to craft the perfect sarcastic retort. She stared at him; he stared back at her. Finally, she let out an exasperated noise and tried to push herself into a standing position. She wanted to stomp out of the room in a flurry of righteous indignation, but her belly was in the way, so it just wasn't happening for her. Instead, she held out her hand with an irritated sigh.

"For crying out loud, Luke!" She waved her hand at him. "Help me up!"

Luke stood, clasped her hand in his and pulled her out of the overstuffed couch.

They were standing close together, too close. She could smell that intoxicating almond scent on his skin. It made her heart race even faster, and she couldn't understand why he wasn't budging. She pushed on his chest.

"Move it, Luke!"

She needed to find something to do, anything, to take her mind off Daniel's arrogant, sarcastic, pain-in-the-ass brother. The farther away from Luke she could get, the better off she'd be.

Luke didn't budge.

"Move!" She reached out and pushed him again. She was being rude and she didn't care. For some reason, no matter what, Luke always brought out the worst in her. Just when she would start to think they had found some common ground, he went and screwed it all up.

This time, Luke turned to the side and let her by. She sent him a slit-eyed look before she lifted up her chin and breezed by him.

Luke watched as Sophia disappeared in the direction of the kitchen. He stood in the same spot for several seconds and felt as if he'd just been mugged. One minute he was enjoying the fire with Sophia, and the next thing he knew she was picking a fight with him. Why did that woman always have to make everything so damned complicated?

Luke looked at Ranger sitting on the edge of the couch cushion. "What the hell just happened here? Can you tell me that?"

Luke sat back down on the couch to contemplate his next move. One option was to not move at all. Normally, with any woman in his life, that's the only option that would have been on the table. He would have stayed put and let them come back to him. They always did come back.

But there wasn't anything *normal* about his situation, and he wasn't dealing with just any woman. He was dealing with Sophia, and she definitely had to be handled with care.

What would Dan do in this situation?

He'd follow after her and eat crow! That's what he'd do. Dan knew how to keep Sophia happy. And now, that was his new mission. Keep Sophia happy.

Luke dropped his head into his hands; that woman was giving him a massive headache. "So, go eat crow, marine."

He dropped Ranger off in the bathroom and popped a pain pill into his mouth before he went to find Sophia in the kitchen. She was sitting at the table, writing in a determined fashion. She didn't bother to acknowledge his presence.

She obviously still wanted to wring his neck.

He tried to break the ice by stating the obvious. He felt like an idiot trying to cajole a woman; it was out of character. "Working on your list?"

Sophia glanced up and narrowed her eyes at him. He had just been trying to lighten the mood, but Sophia looked as if she might want to do him bodily harm.

So much for breaking the ice.

Luke sat down at the table across from her.

"What's on that list of yours, anyway?" Persistence was going to be a key element in this situation. He'd seen Sophia hold a grudge.

Sophia stopped writing and tapped her pen on the table. "Is there something you want?"

Luke rubbed his hands over the top of his shaved head. "God, Sophia, gimme a break, will ya? How was I supposed to know you wanted me to say something?"

She made a face. "Please."

Luke let his arms drop onto the table with a thud. "Okay. How 'bout this? Why don't you tell me what I should have said, because I sure as hell don't know! Tell me what I should say when someone tells me that my face bothers them."

It didn't seem possible, but her eyes narrowed even more. She dropped her head and went back to her list. "Just forget it."

"No. I'm not going to forget it." God, she was a royal pain in the ass! "You wanted to talk about this. Let's talk. I'm telling you flat-out—I didn't know your statement required an answer. You don't want to believe me, that's your problem. But that's the truth. Bottom line."

Sophia chewed on his words for a bit. She glanced up. "You really didn't think you should add something? Really?"

"That's the honest truth. What do you think, that I sit around the campfire with my men singing Kumbaya and talking about our feelings? Come on…I just came out of a war zone, Sophia. You're the shrink. Shouldn't you be able to figure out that there may be an adjustment period for me?"

"You act as if you aren't civilized anymore," she said sullenly. The man did have a good point; there was no denying it.

"Maybe I'm not," Luke said harshly without hesitation. "Because I sure as hell don't know what I should have said to you back there."

Sophia waved the pen in the air. "You could have said something like, 'Gee, Sophia, I didn't know that. I'm sorry that me looking like Daniel is making you feel confused and upset. Thanks for the info. Thanks for sharing.' Something like that. Anything would have been better than *snoring!*"

When the woman had a point, she had a point.

Luke rubbed his hands over his face before he dropped them onto the table in surrender. Emotional conversations had never been his strength; that was a fact. He could have done better with Sophia. He *needed* to do better with Sophia. She deserved it.

"You're right. I could have done a little bit better."

Sophia snorted. "*A lot* better."

"All right. A lot better."

"Substantially better," Sophia added.

Luke got up and pulled a glass out of the cabinet. He filled it up with tap water and chugged it. He turned his back to the counter and crossed his arms over his chest. Sophia was back to her list, and back to ignoring him. It was strange. He hadn't really gotten a good look at her after she came down from her nap. He could see now, in the light of the kitchen, that her eyes were puffy. Sophia had been crying.

He felt like an even bigger jerk, if that was possible. He supposed it *was* possible, because he *did*.

Sophia always seemed so tough. In control. In charge. But right now she appeared vulnerable. He didn't know quite how to deal with this version of the woman he loved. He'd never encountered it before.

"Sophia." He said her name softly.

She ignored him.

Stubborn woman.

"Sophia." He said her name as he always wanted to, like a caress. This grabbed her attention. It got her to look up.

"What?" Still a bite in her tone.

"I'm sorry."

"For what? You don't even know what you did wrong."

"Dammit, Sophia… Can you let a guy apologize without crucifying him?"

Sophia put her pen down. Luke took this as a good sign. "First of all, an apology is useless if you don't know what you're apologizing for. Second of all, watch your mouth."

"First of all, it's not easy switching from marine life to civilian life. I'm sorry about the profanity; all I can say is that I'm working on it." Luke jammed his hands into his front pockets. He lowered his tone back to an acceptable level. "Second of all, I know what I'm apologizing for."

Sophia raised an eyebrow. "Really?"

"Yes."

"What for?"

"For being an insensitive jerk."

Sophia cocked her head and eyed him contempla- tively. "For one thing."

That's the Sophia he knew. The woman didn't give

an inch. Then again, neither did he. This time, he raised his eyebrow at her. "Are you going to let me finish?"

Sophia waved her hand. "By all means. Please do."

Her defenses were still up. Luke could see it plain as day. He had been working to get her defenses down since the moment he had walked through the door, had even managed to make a bit of progress with her, and then in two seconds he was right back to square one. Less than square one!

Nice going, Brand.

Luke knew what he had to do. There wasn't a choice. If he wanted to see that guarded look leave Sophia's eyes, he was going to have to open up to her.

"You know, sensitivity isn't exactly a quality the Marines look for in a man," Luke began.

In spite of herself, Sophia felt like smiling at that comment. She didn't actually do it, but she felt like it.

Luke continued. "So, talking about feelings and sh... stuff like that isn't my area of expertise. Never was, really. Dan was the talker. You know that."

Sophia nodded in agreement.

"I never knew what the heck to say to anyone about anything. Dan always knew. That's why he did most of the talking for the both of us when were kids. Unless the talking that needed to be done had to be done with a fist..." Luke cracked a smile when he said that. "Then, it was my turn to talk for the two of us," he continued. "I guess what I'm trying to say is that I didn't know *what* to say to you, Sophia, so I didn't say anything. From my experience, sometimes it's best just to keep your mouth shut."

Sophia raised her eyebrows again.

"It didn't apply to this particular situation, I admit. Normally, it works out just fine for me. But just because

I didn't know what to say to you doesn't mean I didn't hear what you said, and it doesn't mean that I didn't understand why you said it."

That was the statement that grabbed her total attention. He saw the look in her eyes change. She was listening to every word now.

"I came home early for you, Sophia."

Sophia was rendered speechless for a moment, which was unusual. Even more unusual was a string of more than two sentences coming out of Luke's mouth. And even more unusual than that, was Luke saying that he had come home early for her.

"What do you mean you came home early for me?"

"Do you really think I didn't know you were going to have a hard time being around me? Come on, Sophia...I'm not that much of a jerk. You know that. Or, maybe you don't, which is my fault, no doubt. You're pregnant, you've just lost your husband, and now here comes his twin? That would screw with anyone's head."

Sophia saw something she had never seen in Luke's eyes before. Or, maybe she had never bothered to notice. Compassion. For her.

"So, I came home early, so we could get this—" he moved his hands between them "—this weirdness between us out of the way without an audience."

Sophia rubbed her hands over her belly in a circular motion. It took her a minute to respond. Now it was her turn to not know exactly what to say.

Luke watched her closely. He wanted the trusting look she had given him just this morning to return to her sweet, hazel-green eyes.

"I don't know what to say," she finally admitted.

Luke chuckled. "You might not believe this, but that's happened to me before. Just recently."

He finally got a smile out of Sophia. "Is that so?"

"Yes," he said, relieved to see the stiff set of her jaw soften.

She twisted her wedding ring and studied Luke. "I suppose it never occurred to me that you ever gave me that much thought. You never seemed to like me all that much. I didn't think you'd care one way or the other how I felt about anything, much less something like this. Thank you."

"You're welcome. Am I forgiven now?"

"Of course. What else can I do after all of that?" She waved her hand. "You haven't left me much choice, now have you?"

He winked at her. "That was the plan."

"Well, it worked." For several minutes neither one of them had anything to say. Then Sophia said, "It's really strange being here without him, don't you think?"

Luke nodded. He crossed his arms over his chest and examined the tip of his boot.

Sophia went on. "Everywhere I go in this house, there's a memory of Daniel attached. Weird things bother me, too, things that you wouldn't think would hit you... Like a coffee mug that he used to like to drink out of, or a book in the library he liked to read. And the pictures everywhere, of course." She continued to twist her ring. "The truth is, I don't like being here without him."

In that moment, it hit Sophia that maybe all of this was even harder on Luke than it was on her. She had memories of Daniel in this house only as an adult. Daniel and Luke were born under this roof. Almost all of Luke's memories of this house were intertwined with his brother. Why hadn't she thought of that before? Was she really that insensitive when it came to Luke? Did she think he was a man without feelings?

"I'm sure you feel the same way," she added.

Luke continued to examine his boot. "I expect him to come walking through that door. And when he doesn't..."

"It makes you feel a little crazy inside."

Luke locked eyes with her. "That's right."

"Me, too," Sophia admitted. "Some days it's all I can do to get myself out of bed I feel so lonely for him. But it's not good for the baby. Taking care of our son has actually given me something to fight for. It's given me a purpose other than just myself. Just going to work. This is the biggest job I've ever had to do, and I fully intend to do it right. That's why I refuse to let myself get depressed. Of course, I cry. But I won't let myself wallow. Daniel wouldn't want me to, anyway."

"You're going to be a great mom."

"I hope so," Sophia said. "None of this has been easy. And, honestly, having you here has made it really hard on me. And I know it's not your fault, and I don't expect you to fix it, but whenever I see you, Luke..." She stopped.

"What?" He didn't want her to stop.

"Whenever I see you." Her voice was trembling again. "You look so much like Daniel...I want to hug you. I want to kiss you. I want you to take me in your arms and tell me that you're okay. And I know that sounds nuts, but that's how I feel. I know you're not Daniel, but sometimes..." She stopped again and pressed the heels of her hands into her eyes to stop the tears. She regrouped and started again. "Sometimes, my heart forgets you aren't him, and it's hard not to reach out and touch you. Or, to want you to touch me, for that matter. Does that make any sense to you at all?"

It took all of Luke's willpower not to grab her and crush her in his arms. That's what she needed from him. That's what he wanted to give her. But she would have to come to him. He couldn't risk blowing the truce by overstepping some invisible line. And, if he was honest, he didn't want to know what it could feel like to have Sophia push him away.

"I'm not Daniel," he finally said quietly.

"I know you're not…" she interjected.

He continued on. "And I can't ever be him for you. Even if I could, I wouldn't."

"I know that, Luke," Sophia said, her brow furrowed. "Don't you think I know that?"

"Yes. I do." Luke took his hand out of his pocket and put it on his chest. "But do you know that *I'm* here, Sophia? Do you? I'm right here. Right *here*. My heart's still beating." He emphasized his words by hitting the part of his chest that housed his heart. "I'm still alive and I'm still here. So, if you need someone to hug, Sophia, hug me. You can hug *me*."

Chapter Five

For a split second, Sophia stopped breathing. She didn't move. She didn't blink her eyes. She encouraged her foggy brain to make some sense of the scene unfolding before her. Luke was opening up his heart to her. He was allowing himself to be vulnerable in her presence, and it was something she never expected to happen. He was offering to comfort her, yes. But she knew that he was asking for comfort in return.

Luke needed her. Luke needed comfort from her. Every cell in her body responded to his request. She couldn't have turned him down if she wanted to. And she didn't.

Supporting her belly with one hand, Sophia stood up. Luke had crossed his arms back over his chest, and he was staring at her with a look that Sophia could describe only as suspicious. Why he would be suspicious of her didn't seem to matter. Their eyes were locked as Sophia moved slowly toward him.

She couldn't look away.

She didn't want to look away.

And, for some inexplicable reason, being caught up in Luke's eyes didn't make her uncomfortable. Quite the opposite. It made her feel connected to him in a way she had never known possible. And without thought, without reason, she liked it.

Sophia reached out and tugged on Luke's crossed arms. After a moment of resistance, Luke's arms fell down to his sides. Their eyes were still locked; they were so close that she could see his pupils dilate as she reached out and wrapped her fingers around his wrists. As her fingers made contact with his skin, Sophia watched as his nostrils flared. Her brain registered that he had taken a sharp breath in the moment she touched him. His strange reaction to her touch didn't deter her; her only focus was to hold Luke in her arms. They shared a common sadness. They shared a common loss. It made perfect sense that they should find solace with each other.

Sophia guided Luke away from the counter and stepped into his arms. She wrapped her arms around his waist, pressed her swollen belly against his washboard abdomen and rested her cheek over Luke's rapidly beating heart. His heart was beating so strongly that she could feel the sensation of it against her cheek. She closed her eyes and sighed. His natural scent was so much like Daniel's. It made her feel safe. It made her feel secure. She couldn't figure out where Daniel ended and Luke began, and she didn't care. She just didn't care.

At first, Luke stood stock-still. Every muscle in his

body tensed as Sophia melted against him. He had fantasized about having Sophia in his arms since the first moment he saw her. And now, here she was. He could feel her warmth through the cotton of his shirt. He could smell the sweet lilac scent of her hair. She was so close, he would only have to tilt up her head and he could easily press his lips against her full, soft mouth.

"Hug me back," Sophia said softly.

He felt her words vibrating through the wall of his chest as much as he heard them. Her wish was his command. He wrapped his arms around her shoulders and pulled her tightly into his body. He closed his eyes; his body came alive everywhere Sophia's body touched his. It was intoxicating; Sophia was melting in his arms. The feel of her swollen belly pressed against his body only made the experience more intense, made his desire for her ignite.

He could force himself not to kiss her, but he couldn't stop his body from reacting to hers. Luke tightened his arms around her and buried his face in her hair. One hand moved up to cradle the back of her head, the other moved down to the small of her back. The distance her belly put between their hips saved him; Sophia couldn't feel how his body was reacting to her. His body craved a release that only Sophia could provide. His body wanted something that just wasn't possible.

Luke fought to refocus. He willed his body to cooperate; he shifted his concentration from his frustration to the fluttering feel of Sophia's heart beating against his body. Luke rested his chin on Sophia's head; heard her sigh and relax into his arms even more.

He wanted to push Sophia away; he wanted to pull her closer. He felt as if he had lost his mind in Sophia's arms. Perhaps he had…

"What was that?" Luke untangled himself from Sophia's arms and held her away from him. He looked down at her stomach.

Sophia looked up at him and smiled. "That was Danny." The surprised look on Luke's face made her laugh. "He kicked. You must have felt it because we were close."

"Is that normal?"

The moment was broken; she stepped away from him. "Perfectly normal."

"So, he's okay?" Luke asked.

It was the first time he'd shown real concern for the baby, and it made Sophia soften toward Luke in a way that she hadn't known was possible.

"Sure. He kicks me all the time. And often when I don't *want* him to." She continued to smile up at him. Then, she added with a laugh, "It seems whenever I'm ready to rest, that's when he decides it's time to do somersaults."

Luke's expression changed from concerned to neutral. With a definitive nod, he turned away from Sophia. "I'm going to check on Ranger."

"Okay." She tried very hard to stop her disappointment from reflecting in her tone. For whatever reason, Sophia didn't want this moment with Luke to end.

"I'll be back," Luke threw over his shoulder as he disappeared into the hall.

For a moment, Sophia didn't move. She had just shared an extremely intimate hug with Luke, and the experience had left her feeling odd. Luke hadn't even hugged her at the wedding. He had shaken her hand, for crying out loud. And now this? It was a shock to the system.

The truth was undeniable: she had loved every minute she had been in Luke's arms. He was strong and warm and hugged her back as if he meant it. For a split second, she had imagined she was with Daniel, but surprisingly, that moment was fleeting. There was no denying Luke. He was a force to be reckoned with.

Danny kicked her again and it drew her attention back to her baby. She rubbed her hands over her belly and smiled down at her rambunctious son. "Like father like son, eh, Danny boy? You just can't stand it if you aren't the center of attention."

Luke let Ranger out of the bathroom, then went to his room and closed the door firmly behind him. He locked the door and rested his forehead against it. He had to get out of the kitchen fast. His body refused to stop thinking about making love to Sophia, and the last thing he needed was for Sophia to notice the obvious bulge in his pants.

There wouldn't be any way to explain that one away.

Luke shut the blinds, shut the adjoining bathroom door and spread out on the bed. The kitten curled up in a ball on the pillow, while Luke let out a frustrated growl. His body wasn't giving up. He was still aroused, and it was starting to hurt.

A cold shower was the only plausible solution.

Luke stripped off his clothes and let the frigid water pelt his skin. Luke looked down at his body in disbelief. His problem refused to go away. What had Sophia done to him?

"Come on!" he said through gritted teeth. He closed his eyes and leaned back so the water could pound him on the chest.

If this didn't work, he was going to have to get rid of it the old-fashioned way. He had been without a woman for too long; he wanted Sophia too much. Under the circumstances, it was a horrible combination.

It took longer than he would have liked, but the freezing water did the trick. Luke stepped out of the shower, dried off, yanked on some boxer-briefs and flopped back onto the bed. He didn't bother to finish dressing or bandaging his wound. He just wanted a minute to get his head straight. Being around Sophia was driving him nuts. More times than he'd like to admit, he had thought about walking away from her. Anything would be easier than this. He'd rather be dropped into a hot zone from a perfectly good plane one hundred times a day than spend the next week sorting things out with Sophia. It was just too damn hard not to let her see how he felt about her. It was a minute-by-minute struggle not to just get it out in the open and let the chips fall where they may.

But he knew he couldn't do that. He had to keep himself under control no matter what. His feelings couldn't matter. He had his whole family to consider.

He had Dan's son to consider.

Luke rubbed his hands over his face. That kick was the first time it had truly sunk in that Sophia was carrying a real person inside her. Of course, he could see that she was pregnant; he could see the fullness of her breasts, the roundness of her belly. Her face was fuller, yet still incredibly beautiful. He could easily see the changes, but for some reason, it took *feeling* it, feeling the baby move, for the whole thing to become real.

That kick came at the right time. It helped him get his head clear, helped him get his brain back on track and back into reality.

As Luke was lulled to sleep by the rhythmic sound of Ranger purring in his ear, he felt more determined than ever not to screw things up with Sophia. More than ever, Luke wanted to get to know that little boy who had just given him a swift kick in the gut. That kick had done more than just wake Luke up; that kick had made him fall in love for the second time in his life. Luke was head over heels crazy about little Danny. Bottom line.

Sophia checked her cell phone. One missed call. It must have gone straight to voice mail; it hadn't bothered to ring. "Stupid reception," she said bitterly as she punched the buttons and pulled up her missed calls list.

"Allie." Sophia read the name out loud. Allie was her best friend and one of her most valuable "baby" assets. Allie had three children of her own and had an extremely busy career as a speech-language pathologist. She was Sophia's inspiration to find a balance between motherhood and work in her own life.

Sophia dialed Allie's number on the landline and waited while it rang.

Allie picked up the phone on the third ring. "Where have you been? Why didn't you answer your phone? You're supposed to have it with you at *all times!* All times!" That was just like Allie; forceful, to the point. "I've been worried sick, thank you very much. You could've been carried away by thieves, carved up and left on the side of the road, for all I knew!"

"Thanks for the graphic image, Al." Sophia leaned against the counter. "The reception is a nightmare here. This is the home phone number. Use that if you need to get ahold of me."

Allie retorted, "Thanks for making me panic, lady! I was just about to make a call."

Sophia smiled. "Who were you going to call?"

"I don't know," Allie snapped, but Sophia knew her

well enough to know she was starting to soften. "There has to be someone you can call out there in the middle of absolutely nowhere." According to Allie, if there wasn't an outlet mall within a ten-mile radius, the place wasn't civilized. "Could the National Guard reach you out there?"

Sophia laughed. Allie always made her laugh. "I'm in Montana, Al...not the jungle. Half of Hollywood lives out here."

"What's that supposed to mean? Does that make it safe? Is L.A. safe? I don't think so. But you've gotten me way off the point. You're out there, in the middle of nowhere, pregnant, *alone*..."

Sophia interjected. "Not alone."

There was a pause on the other end of the line. "Is the family back early?"

"No," Sophia said, dragging out the word for a while.

"Who's there?" Allie asked suspiciously. "You haven't picked up a hitchhiker or are feeding some homeless guy, are you?"

"Okay... That's something *you* would totally do..."

Allie chuckled. "That's true. I would. But I'm not eight months pregnant and stranded in the middle of nowhere." Every time Allie said the phrase "in the middle of nowhere," she had to really emphasize it. "Who's out there with you?"

"Luke's here."

Another pause. "Luke? As in Daniel's brother, Luke?"

"Yes."

"You're kidding."

"No. He showed up the day after Thanksgiving."

She didn't have to see Allie to know that her eyebrows were raised at the juicy news. "Wow. So how's that going? If I remember correctly, the two of you are like oil and water."

Sophia smiled. She supposed her rocky relationship with Luke wasn't exactly a well-kept secret. "We still are...sort of. He's making an effort to get along with me..."

"Are you making an effort to get along with him?" Allie interjected.

"Yes. Of course. For my son's sake, if for nothing else."

"You know what...?"

"What?"

"I'm really glad to hear it. Luke could be incredibly important in your son's life. Your son has an advantage that most children who lose a father don't have. His uncle is a twin. Danny can actually see what his father looks like, what he sounds like, and I have no doubt that Luke is full of stories about Daniel."

"You're right. I think Luke feels the same way. And, I have to tell you, there's a lot about Luke I never knew...."

"Like...?"

"Like he isn't as much of a...jerk...as I once thought. He's actually quite..." Sophia paused to think of the right word to fill in the blank. "Nice."

"I never thought he was a jerk, anyway. He was always very polite to me. And I loved to see him in his uniform. Handsome. If I hadn't been married at the time, I would have insisted that man show me a good time...."

"Allie!" Sophia said, caught off guard. "Really?"

"Oh, please...like you haven't noticed how handsome Luke is? You married his twin."

"Yeah, but I never really thought of Luke in that

way. Daniel was the handsome one, at least to me he was. Besides, Luke was always a pain in my neck…."

"Like the little boy who pulls on the girls' pigtails in school…"

"What's that supposed to mean?"

"You know… When we were little, boys were always mean to the girls they liked. It's the same with Luke. I always thought he had a thing for you."

Sophia's stomach twisted into a knot. "That's crazy. Luke doesn't have a thing for me. Trust me! I would know."

"No, you wouldn't. You're blind as a bat when it comes to stuff like that. You have absolutely no radar for that sort of thing whatsoever. I, on the other hand, do. And, I tell you, Luke has always had a thing for you. I saw him giving you 'the look' a couple of times."

"What 'look'?"

"*The* look. Like he's trying to imagine what you look like naked kind of look!"

That made Sophia laugh out loud. "Now I know you're delusional. Have you been getting enough rest? Are you sleep deprived? Taking any new medications I should be aware of?"

"You can laugh all you want, Soph. But I'm serious. Luke has feelings for you."

Sophia shrugged off Allie's words. Usually her friend did have an uncanny ability to spot stuff like that, but this time she had to be way off base. Luke didn't have a thing for her. No way.

Allie spent the next half hour giving Sophia Boston highlights, which only made Sophia more homesick for her life back home. She couldn't wait to get back to her city and make a new life with her son.

"Tell Luke 'hi' for me. Oh, and tell him the next time

he's in town to bring his uniform and I'll let him take me out on a date," Allie said with a laugh. "You have to love a man in uniform. And I've always had a soft spot for marines. Especially sexy marines like Luke."

For some inexplicable reason, Sophia's gut clenched at the thought of Luke and Allie dating. Allie was just joking around, but she didn't like the idea one bit. She'd never cared one iota before; she sure as heck shouldn't care now! And yet…she did.

To Allie she said, "I'll tell him."

To herself, she said, *get a grip, Sophia!*

After she hung up, Sophia went into the library and sat down in her favorite double chair. She pulled a blanket over her legs and stared into the fireplace. It was chilly in the room, and she found herself wishing Luke would reappear and build a fire for the both of them. She wanted the warmth of a fire and Luke's company. A couple of times she thought about getting up and building the fire herself, but she didn't want to take the job away from Luke. He seemed to like filling that role, and she enjoyed watching him.

As she waited for Luke, her mind drifted to the conversation she had earlier with Allie. She still couldn't understand where the jealousy had come from, but it was undeniable. And for some inexplicable reason she hadn't told Allie about the hug she had shared with Luke. That wasn't like her at all; normally she confided stuff like that to her best friend. This time, she hadn't. She had wanted to keep the moment she had shared with Luke and her *reaction* to the moment to herself.

"You look like you could use a fire." Luke walked into the room followed by Ranger.

Sophia leaned her head back against the chair. "I was hoping you'd come down soon."

"Why didn't you come get me?"

"I didn't want to disturb you. Figured you were resting." She shrugged one shoulder. "And I was being incredibly lazy. I could have easily done it myself...."

Luke leaned his cane against the couch before he threw a couple of logs into the fireplace. He interrupted her. "You shouldn't have to do stuff like that while I'm here. That's my job. If you need something, don't hesitate to ask. Are we clear?"

"Okay," she agreed with a faint smile. His bossy tone, which normally set her teeth on edge, didn't seem to bother her this time. It felt good to have Luke looking after her. She twisted her wedding ring as she watched Luke build the fire.

After the fire was lit, Luke sat down on the couch. "Listen, I hope I didn't overstep some invisible line earlier. I'm trying to stay on your good side."

"You didn't. Trust me. If I knew you were hug-friendly, I might have attacked you the first day you arrived!"

That got a half smile and a chuckle out of Luke. He winked at her, and something about that wink made her heart skip a beat. "Consider me officially open for business."

Chapter Six

Sophia couldn't seem to get enough of Luke's company. After they enjoyed the fire they went for a walk, which was absolute heaven for her. She loved the outdoors, and with Luke's arm to hold on to she had navigated the icy porch stairs, and the icy patches on the ground, without a second thought. She hadn't felt that invigorated in a week, and by the time they had returned to the house she had a renewed sense of purpose. The walls didn't seem to be closing in on her any longer.

Now that it was just the two of them it was easy to see how compatible they were together. And they seemed to gravitate toward the same part of the house: they both loved to sit in the library in front of the fire. So, after dinner, Luke headed toward the library to throw some more logs on the fire, and she found herself hurrying her movements to get back to Luke more quickly.

She could imagine Daniel looking down on her and smiling right now. He would have a hard time believing his eyes, but he would have been thrilled. Next to her, Luke had been Daniel's best friend, and it always hurt him that the two of them didn't get along.

"It took this to bring us together, my love," Sophia said softly as she pulled the mugs out of the cabinet. "I wish you were here to see it."

But, the truth was, if Daniel had been here, she and Luke would still be keeping their distance from each other. It had taken a tragedy; it had taken them losing the most important person in both of their lives for them to put aside their petty differences.

Better late than never, she supposed.

"Here ya go." Sophia walked into the library; she carried a full cup in each hand. Ranger jumped out from the side of the couch and batted at her feet with his little paws. She stopped, surprised, and the liquid in the cups sloshed.

"Here, I got it…." Luke reached out for his cup.

Sophia shook her head and smiled at the kitten. "What are you doing, stinker?"

Luke sank down into his spot on the couch and took a sip of his black coffee. As usual, Sophia had it right. The fact that she remembered his likes and dislikes didn't surprise him anymore; it just made him feel good. It let him know, for the first time, that he was a part of Sophia's life. He mattered, and had always mattered enough for her to take notice of, and remember, small details about him.

Sophia sank down into her favorite chair across from the couch and put up her feet. The fire was just starting to crackle and she could feel the warmth of the blaze on her face as it took the chill off the room. "Ah. This is perfect. Thank you." She took a sip of her tea before she added, "This is becoming a regular thing for us, isn't it?"

"Seems that way." Luke's eyes were on her in the dimly lit room. "Thanks for the coffee."

"You're welcome." She heard the sincerity in her own voice. She had actually started to enjoy bringing small pleasures into Luke's life. At first it was just to stave off boredom, but it had quickly become something she enjoyed doing. That made her smile.

Luke noticed the small smile and asked, "What?"

Sophia shook her head softy. "I was just thinking about how civil we are with each other now. We've been like oil and water for years, and now..."

"Not so much," Luke filled in.

"Yes. Not so much," Sophia said before she brought her cup up to her lips and blew on the hot liquid. "Daniel would be proud of us, don't you think?"

"Dan would be proud," Luke agreed. "Speechless actually, which would've been a switch."

"True." Sophia laughed.

As Sophia slowly sipped on her tea and focused her eyes on the fire, Luke focused his eyes on her. His eyes traveled over every feature of her face; he loved the way the firelight cast a golden hue across her honey skin. She was the most beautiful woman he had ever seen. He loved every angle of her face, every laugh line around her eyes; the quickness of her smile. As far as he was concerned, Sophia had always looked like an angel. And he adored her.

The harsh truth was that he had imagined himself in this very situation with Sophia many times over the past ten years. Of course, in his fantasies, she was never across the room from him; she'd be right next to him, where he could keep his hands on her at all times.

This fantasy come to life was more bitter than sweet, because his brother was gone. But nothing would change the fact that he loved being with Sophia. And, for him, being with her now put a much-needed salve on the wound that Dan's death had carved into his heart. Now that baby boy Sophia was carrying was another much-needed salve. He already loved the boy as his own.

"What are you thinking about?" Sophia had turned her face toward him, and now their eyes were locked.

"Dan."

A small smile lifted her bow-shaped lips. "Me, too. What were you thinking?"

"I was wondering if he knew he was going to be a father."

Sophia took a deep breath in and felt her gut clench. It took her a minute to compose herself before she gave a small shake of her head. "He didn't. It's strange how life works out, isn't it? We hadn't planned on having a family until he was finished with his Ph.D. We had everything planned out, you know? Everything. Then, the next thing I know, Daniel comes home and says he's joined the army. Just like that." She snapped her fingers. "I was *literally* blown away. And furious, to tell you the truth." She glanced away from the fire to Luke for a split second. "I've never been that angry in my life! And, believe me, I let him know about it every chance I got. I wish I hadn't now."

"You can't blame yourself for that, Soph. If I had been within arm's length of him, I would have personally strangled him myself! I don't know what the *hell* he was thinking."

"I know you're right, but I can't seem to forgive myself for that fight. I play it over and over in my head, and sometimes I can't sleep. I know I shouldn't drive myself nuts like that, but my brain just won't give it a rest. I said some pretty horrible things to him that night. Things that I should never have said…"

She paused her story for a minute while she pressed her fingers to the corner of her eyes. After a minute she shook her head and continued. "He'd never even mentioned joining the army, Luke. Not *once,* in all the years we had been together. It was like boom, boom, boom." Sophia hit the arm of the chair with her hand. "One minute he had joined, and the next minute he was gone to officer training. Then, the next thing I know, he's saying he's going to Iraq. It was like being on a rollercoaster ride against my will and I couldn't get off!" She looked at Luke with a slightly accusatory set to her mouth. "He never told you why he joined?"

"No," Luke said flatly, but she heard anger creep into his voice. "I was hoping you had an answer to that question."

She crossed her arms over her chest and stared sullenly into the fire. "Well, I don't." She could hear that same old bitterness in her tone, never far from the surface. "I thought if he had told anyone why he did something that *crazy,* something that totally out of character, it would've been you. If it hadn't been me, at least he could have told you." She forced the bitterness that had bubbled up back down. It was pointless to be bitter, so she squashed it. Temporarily if not permanently. "I asked him, of course. I was like a bloody broken record…."

Luke made a noise in the back of his throat. "I bet you were…."

"But time and time again he wouldn't give a straight answer. He kept on saying that he thought it was his duty as an American, which is exactly the kind of crap I used to hear you say about being a marine." She held up her hand to him. "No offense."

"None taken."

"I even blamed you, but he denied you had anything to do with it…."

"He didn't tell me until after he'd already done it. I've never been that damned angry in my life…."

"I knew in my heart that you hadn't talked him into it, you know." She shrugged one shoulder. "I just wanted someone to blame. For a while that someone was you. Sorry."

"No apology needed. I blamed myself. Why shouldn't you?" Luke asked angrily.

"It wasn't your fault." Her reply was quick and firm. "Daniel had a mind of his own. Why he did it, none of us will ever know. But, in the end, it was his choice, his price to pay. Anyway, we didn't have many pleasant conversations right up to the time he left. I couldn't accept what he had done, and I picked fights with him every chance I got."

"You were scared."

"I was. But I still feel guilty about it. We fought at the end more than not. But he blindsided me, and that wasn't fair either. We discussed everything, *everything,* in our marriage, or at least I thought we did. And here I was so smug about my marriage whenever my friends would complain about their relationships. I never had anything bad to say about Daniel." She smiled. "Other than the fact that he snored and hogged the bed."

She rested her head in her hand and took a minute to imagine Daniel in their bed: naked, lean, totally sexy.

Luke watched the expression on her face change from sweet to almost sensual. The lids of her eyes dropped, her full lips parted, and he could see that her breathing had deepened almost imperceptibly. But he noticed. He noticed everything about her.

"But you still never got it out of him," he said to jump-start the conversation again.

Sophia slid her eyes toward him. "Hmm? Oh, no. I never did. The only decision he ever made without me, and it turned out to be the most important decision of our lives." Her hand moved over her stomach. "All of our lives."

"And the baby?" Luke prodded.

Sophia's hand stilled and rested on her stomach. "Daniel surprised me with a visit right before he shipped out. I hadn't been expecting him, we were out of condoms, and one thing led to another...."

"You're kidding..."

The look on Luke's face was comical in its surprise and she couldn't help but laugh at the situation. "My husband had just shipped out. Why would I restock the condoms?"

Luke leaned back and propped his hands on the top of his head. He nodded toward her stomach. "It's a good thing you didn't. Now we have a piece of Daniel."

Every time Luke said something positive about her son, it made her soften toward him. She couldn't help herself. "Just think, if he hadn't come home for a visit, I wouldn't be having his son right now."

"Or, if he had stopped off for condoms."

"Touché. But I think I'll keep that little fact from Danny... Why give him a complex, right?"

"Good call."

"You know, I have no idea why I told you that…I haven't told anyone that story, not even my best friend!"

"Your secret is safe with me."

She narrowed her eyes playfully at him. "Do you swear?"

Luke reached down and made an X over his heart. "Cross my heart. Dan Junior won't hear it from me."

"I'd appreciate it," Sophia bantered back. She was beginning to understand Luke's sense of humor. It was irreverent and it made her laugh. It felt good to laugh, and with Luke, she had been laughing wholeheartedly for the first time since Daniel's death.

After a moment, when they both stopped laughing, Luke prompted her to continue. "So, he didn't know you were pregnant?"

"No. I didn't know myself until I was two months along. By then…"

"He was gone," Luke filled in for her as her words trailed off. Dan wasn't made for combat. He had been the sensible one of the two of them. He had been the brains; Luke was the brawn. He had been killed in an explosion soon after he had arrived in Iraq.

"Yes," Sophia said softly. "By then he was gone." Sophia paused and then glanced over at Luke. "Don't worry, Captain, I'm not going to start crying."

"If you won't, maybe I will," Luke said dryly.

Instead, it was Ranger who cried at Luke from beside the couch; Luke scooped him up and the kitten happily curled up on Luke's chest, closed his eyes and promptly fell asleep.

Sophia pulled the blanket tight under her chin and curled up in the chair. Once again, little Danny insisted on jamming his feet underneath her ribs; it felt as if he were using her ribs as a springboard in order to do a full somersault.

"Hey," she said as she poked the baby in her belly with her fingers. "Why do you have to be so rough in there?"

"Like father, like son," Luke murmured, his eyes closed.

"Exactly," Sophia said. Then added, "Like uncle, like nephew, too, I think."

Luke said proudly, "Brand boys." He moved his head sideways and looked at her.

"You know," Sophia continued, "one of the strangest things about this whole pregnancy thing is that the minute I stop moving, that's when he decides he wants to have a little party in there. It'd be nice if we could both be still at the same time!"

"That'd be too easy," Luke said, and then, after a brief pause, "could I feel him moving? You know, like I did before?"

Sophia shrugged. "It could happen, I'm sure, but another strange thing about it is that for some reason, when someone touches my stomach, he stops moving. Thank God for the internet so I know all of this stuff and don't freak out when it happens."

"I'd like to feel him moving around again."

"You sound like you love him."

"I do," Luke said easily and without hesitation. "Dan's son is my son, too."

If she hadn't sworn off hormonal crying, this would have been a perfect time to indulge. Luke's words made her feel more secure than she had felt in a long time. For some reason, at that moment, it seemed to her that she wasn't going to have to raise little Daniel without a strong male influence.

"I'm glad," Sophia finally said once she felt safe to talk without crying. "I'm really glad to hear that."

"I know you can't trust it yet, Sophia, but I'm here for you. That's a fact."

They spent the rest of the evening in comfortable companionship. She asked Luke to tell her Daniel stories, and after a good dose of strong coffee, Luke told one story after another until the caffeine started to wear off. Sophia had closed her eyes while Luke talked, and occasionally allowed herself to drift into a place where she could imagine that Daniel was in the room talking to her. Luke's voice was so similar to Daniel's that it wasn't hard to do; in that moment, she had Daniel back with her, and it was priceless.

She didn't know when she fell asleep, but the next thing she knew, Luke was gently shaking her leg to wake her up. She slowly opened her eyes and blinked at him.

"Did I fall asleep?"

"Yes," Luke said wryly. "So much for my riveting storytelling."

Sophia glanced over at the fire. It had died down and Luke had the grate back in place. "Sorry."

He offered his hand. "You ready for bed?"

"You're not mad, are you?" She held out her hand.

"Please," he said as he engulfed her hand with his strong, warm fingers. He pulled her up. "I'm used to women falling asleep on me."

She wrinkled her forehead at him and said groggily, "Now I'm gonna say, 'Please…give me a break, Captain Brand.' You had women crawling all over you in college. I'm sure it's not any different now."

Just not the one I wanted to crawl all over me.

He offered her his arm and out loud, he said, "There were a lot of women with very bad taste at that school."

She took his arm and frowned at him playfully. "That's a *horrible* thing to say. I thought most of your girlfriends were really pretty and nice. Except for that cheerleader you dated, remember her? She was a real tramp."

He looked down at her. "Why don't you tell me how you really feel about her?"

She frowned. "Well, she was. But, other than her, I thought you had really good taste. Honestly, I never understood why you didn't settle down with one of them eventually."

Because none of them were you.

"I wanted to save them the trouble of divorcing me," Luke said dryly as he looked over his shoulder and whistled for Ranger. "Come on, little man."

The kitten trilled, stuck his tail straight up in the air and raced to catch up with them.

Sophia liked the feeling of having her hand on his forearm. She liked the feeling of walking beside him. And it wasn't just because he reminded her of Daniel. This time, this particular evening, she discovered that she was enjoying walking next to Luke; standing this close to Luke, just for Luke.

She was just too tired to try to analyze it. It just *was*.

A question was formulating in her fuzzy head, and the curious side of her brain was fighting with the cautious side. Finally, the curious side won out and she tried to sound nonchalant when she asked the question. "Are you seeing anyone now?"

She didn't sound half as casual as she would have liked. And, for some reason, her heart was beginning to thump in the most annoying way as she anticipated his answer.

Luke cocked an eyebrow at her as he helped her up the stairs. "Why do you ask?"

Sophia shrugged as if she couldn't care less. "No reason, really. Other than the fact that my friend Allie... remember her?" Luke nodded. "Well, I told her you were here and she said that she thought you were handsome...."

"Ah...I see. You're trying to fix me up..." There was a bite in his tone that made her glance at his strong, handsome profile.

"Well..." Sophia said slowly, "if you aren't with anyone...and she's single..."

"Allie is a beautiful woman," Luke said easily.

Sophia's eyes quickly found his face again. There was something in his tone she didn't like. He sounded interested, and the compliment made her feel a pang of jealousy.

"Yes, she is," she agreed quickly, and meant it.

"And a great mom," he added.

Another pang. "The best. You should give her a call sometime. She's single now and..."

He cut her off. "I'm not in the market for a woman like Allie."

Relief flooded her body. "Why not?"

"Allie's the type of woman you settle down with."

"And you aren't ready to settle down?"

"No," he said decisively. "I'm not."

She just couldn't give up the conversation, even when she knew she should leave it well enough alone. "But you do date...?"

"What's with all of the questions about my love life?" Luke evaded the question.

"What's with the secrecy?" she countered, and wondered if her cheeks were starting to redden with embarrassment.

"No secrecy. I have several women who I…keep company with."

She knew exactly what "keeping company" meant. And why not? Luke was an unmarried, red-blooded, American male. Why shouldn't he be involved sexually with women? And yet, she didn't like the idea at all.

At the top of the stairs, Sophia's brain was whirling with possible images of the women in Luke's life. Who were these women? How many were there? How often did he see them?

She shouldn't care one bit if he was seeing ten thousand women! She had zero reason to be jealous. No right. None whatsoever.

But she was so filled up with it at the moment that she was surprised her eyes hadn't turned a bright shade of green.

She should keep her mouth shut, and yet she couldn't seem to do just that. Nor could she keep the disapproving tone out of her voice when she asked, "So, what is it…a 'woman in every port' kind of thing?"

Luke was examining her with a curious, slightly amused expression on his handsome face. "Something like that," he said easily. Too easily for her taste.

Sophia tried to stop herself from frowning and failed. Then she managed to muster a tired smile. "Good night, Luke."

He had the distinct feeling that he had hurt her in some way, but he would be damned if he knew what it was. He didn't want her to leave on a bad note, not after such a great day together. "You don't approve?"

She paused in her doorway. "It's your life, Luke. Who am I to judge?"

"Your opinion matters."

"It shouldn't," she said wearily as she started to shut her door.

"I feel like I've done something to upset you, but for the life of me, I can't figure out what it is...."

Sophia mustered a weak smile; she was acting like a lunatic. "You haven't done anything, Luke. Your personal life is really none of my business. I was just passing along the message from Allie."

"So, you aren't mad?" Luke asked.

"No. I'm not mad at you, Luke. I'm exhausted, pregnant and just a little bit nuts. I'll feel better after I get some sleep. Good night."

"Good night." Luke watched as Sophia disappeared into her room before he went into his. By the time he made it into his room, Sophia had already closed the adjoining bathroom door and was preparing for bed. He sat on the edge of the bed and listened to her go through her nightly routine. He liked being this close to her, and something as simple as listening to her prepare for bed gave him a sense of intimacy with the woman he loved. There had been a lot of women in his life; he loved women and they seemed to gravitate toward him. But he'd never found another woman who could replace Sophia in his heart. He had tried. Many times. He had always failed.

Sophia crawled into bed feeling exhausted and confused. Luke kept on tying her into knots in one way or another. She was hoping in time things would make sense, because right now they didn't. She listened as Luke prepared for bed and wondered about the women in his life.

She didn't have any doubt that they were all gorgeous creatures. Most likely, they were exotic women who had great bodies and lots of brains. Luke always wanted the entire package and he was a man who always got what he wanted. The image of a willowy brunette with pouty lips, blue eyes and a Ph.D. was the last unfortunate image she had in her head before she drifted off to sleep.

The sound of a man's voice jarred her awake.

Sophia jerked her head off the pillow and stared confused into the darkened room. The digital clock on the nightstand read 2:15 a.m. She had been asleep for several hours.

Had she dreamt the male voice?

She was just about to think that the voice *had* been a part of a dream when she heard it again.

It was Luke's voice. The words were unintelligible, but the tone was unmistakable. He was yelling and his voice was commanding, urgent.

She pushed herself out of bed as quickly as she could and crossed to his room through the bathroom. She flipped on the bathroom light and tapped on the door lightly.

"Luke?"

He didn't answer, but she heard him mumble something she couldn't understand.

"Luke?" She tapped louder this time. No answer.

Impatient, she opened the door and peaked inside the room. Luke was sprawled out on the bed in his underwear. One arm was flung over his forehead and the other dangled off the side of the bed.

"Luke?" She said his name again, and walked quietly over to the bed. As she got closer, she could see that his body was covered with a thin sheen of sweat; his face was flushed.

Concerned, she stopped at the edge of the bed. He was still mumbling; she strained to make out the words.

"Luke," she said more forcefully as she reached out her hand to touch his arm.

In an instant, Luke's eyes popped open and his fingers closed over her wrist. She could see by the confused look in his eyes that he didn't recognize her. His fingers were like a steel band around her wrist; it didn't hurt, but she couldn't move away either. She was trapped, and if this hadn't been Luke holding her wrist so firmly, she would have been afraid. But this was Luke, so she had nothing to fear.

Chapter Seven

Luke was looking at her so strangely; she'd never seen this look in his eyes before. It was unnerving. He still held her wrist in his hand. The pressure didn't hurt, but she had the distinct sensation that it wouldn't take much for Luke to change that situation.

"It's Sophia, Luke," she said quietly; she kept her tone even and calm.

The look in his eyes shifted; he recognized her. "What are you doing in here?"

"You were having a…" She paused to find the right word. "A nightmare, I think."

Luke's eyes moved to his hand on her wrist. He released her as if he had been burned.

Instead of taking a step back, she leaned forward and touched his forehead. His body was tense, the muscles coiled as if he was about to spring into action. He could have avoided her hand, but he didn't.

"My God, Luke, you're burning up. Do you feel sick? Is it your leg?"

Her cool hand felt so good on his forehead, it took a minute for him to remember himself. He could distinctly see the outline of her full breasts barely concealed behind the thin material of her nightgown. Her hair, long and loose, drifted over one shoulder. She smelled so good; so fresh and clean. He wanted to reach up and bury his hand in her hair, bring her face close to his, breathe her in.

Luke pushed himself up and swung his legs over the side. Sophia stepped sideways and let him by as he stood up. He marched over to the bathroom, with a slight limp, and ignored the cane. He jerked on the faucet, bent over the sink and splashed the frigid water on his face and over his head, which washed away the sweat from his brow and neck.

Sophia watched him from the doorway. After a minute, she reached over and pulled a hand towel from the cupboard and handed it to him.

"Here." She shook the towel.

"Thanks." This was said gruffly as he wiped the towel over his head, his neck and his chest. Sophia didn't avert her eyes as he dried himself off. It didn't take much for the psychologist in her to figure out what she had just witnessed. In fact, before she had left Boston for Montana, she had counseled several veterans; she was acutely aware of how active combat could impact a person's psyche. She wondered if Luke was aware of post-traumatic stress, or if he had chosen to ignore any negatives that came along with his blind dedication to the Marines.

Luke caught her eye; he rubbed the towel over his chest one last time before he threw it over the tub. They stood face-to-face, neither one of them spoke, neither one of them moved. There was something raw and intense in the way he examined her. She could feel the heat of his body radiating onto her skin.

"Did I hurt you?" he demanded, finally. His tone was commanding, but she detected the underlying concern in the question.

"No," she said quickly. "Don't be ridiculous. You would never hurt me."

Luke's face hardened; his jaw clenched. "You have no idea what I'm capable of."

She could tell that he was done with the conversation, but Sophia didn't budge. She scoffed. "Yes, I do. You would never hurt me. Not ever."

He took in a long, deep breath through his nose while he examined her through narrowed, contemplative eyes. In the light, his eyes had turned a dark, sapphire blue, and she found it impossible to look away. Whenever he caught her up in his gaze, she became mesmerized by the power, confidence and control that lurked behind his shocking blue eyes.

"Finally," he said. "You'd be wise not to sneak up on me again."

Her hands went immediately to her hips. Defensively, she retorted, "I didn't sneak up on you, Brand. I came to check up on you. There's a huge difference."

"Either way." Luke stepped toward his bedroom, but she still didn't feel inclined to move.

"Don't you think we should talk about what happened here? There is obviously something wrong that needs to be addressed...."

"Christ, woman!" Luke snapped. "Why can't you ever just give it a rest? Why can't you ever just let something go? I'm not one of your patients. Don't psycho-analyze me to death!"

"I'm not *psychoanalyzing you to death*. I'm trying to help. Perhaps you need to acknowledge the fact that being a marine can have some negative consequences." As the words came out of her mouth, she could see the muscles tighten in his chest and neck. The man was truly unreasonable when it came to his career.

"My life is on the line every day… Death is a pretty serious negative consequence, don't you think?"

"Yes, I do, and I…"

Luke's face had become a granite mask again, but there was fire in his eyes. "So, what the hell is it that you don't think I know about the negatives of being a marine?"

"First of all, don't interrupt me. Second of all, don't curse at me. And third of all, some of my patients be-lieve it would be easier to die in combat than to live with the memories for the rest of their lives!" Now her voice was raised, and she felt her heart as it pumped harder in her chest.

"You just like pushing my buttons, don't you? Is that it? You just can't stand it if we're getting along, can you? Perhaps you're the one with the problem here. Did you ever think of that? Why don't *you* stand here and get some self-reflection time in while I get back to bed?"

"I'm not pushing anything…." Sophia felt her own jaw set.

"Good. Then, if you don't mind stepping aside—" Luke stepped toward his bedroom again "—I'd like to get some more shut-eye."

Sophia crossed her arms over her chest, but she moved out of his way.

"You should go back to bed, too," he said in that commanding tone that she had always hated. What in the world had *ever* given Luke the impression he could boss her around? He gave her a cursory once-over with his eyes that made her thumping heart skip a beat, partly from irritation, partly from some other emotion she'd rather not admit to. "You need your rest."

"I *was* in bed. I would still be in bed, *asleep,* if you hadn't awakened me!" she snapped. The man had the audacity to tell her to self-reflect when it was *his* nightmare that had jarred her out of her own sleep. The man was *infuriating!*

Luke sat on the edge of his bed and grunted his displeasure. He looked as if he were sculpted out of marble; every muscle was hard, defined, and rippled with his slightest move. There wasn't an ounce of fat on his body; the man was built to fight, there was no doubt about it.

"Go back to bed, Sophia." He gave a shake of his head and said quietly, "You're concerned; I get it. But I've got it handled. You don't need to worry."

"I don't need to worry?" She repeated it as if she hadn't quite heard him correctly. "You wake me up out of a sound sleep…you're shouting, you're burning up…"

Luke interrupted her with a low growl in the back of his throat. She clamped her mouth shut and watched him through narrowed, irritated eyes. She wasn't going to get anywhere with Luke tonight. It was time to quit. But she sure as hell wasn't about to let it drop for good. Luke should at least know her better than to expect that.

"Fine." This was said in a disgruntled tone. "I'm going back to bed."

"Sleep well." Now that he had his way, he was being polite.

"Bug off, Brand," she snapped as she shut the door behind her.

Sophia woke up feeling lousy. Of course, being a typical female, she had been awake for the majority of the night stewing over what had happened with Luke. She had changed positions, meditated and even tried to count sheep; nothing had worked. The more she tried to sleep and failed, the more irritated she felt toward Luke. Her irritation only increased when she heard him snoring from the other room. He had awakened her from a sound sleep, yet he fell back asleep with no problem, while she spent the rest of the night tossing and turning. Typical man!

Sophia shuffled into the bathroom and looked at her reflection. Her eyes were baggy and her face looked puffy. She leaned forward for a closer look, frowned at her reflection as she pulled down the skin on her cheeks, and made a displeased noise.

She broke from her usual routine of a morning yoga stretch, brushed her teeth, threw on a comfortable sweat suit and yanked her hair into a haphazard ponytail. She had been up all night thinking about Luke and she was determined to talk to him about what happened.

Whether he liked it or not.

Sophia opened the door to her room, noted that Ranger was already on the loose and the door to Luke's room was ajar. She knew he was an early riser, but since he had been home, she had beaten him downstairs every day. She found him in the family room; the cane was propped against the wall and Luke was bending over one of the boxes filled with his mother's Christmas decorations.

"You're up early," she said from the doorway.

He looked annoyingly well rested.

"You're up late," he retorted easily; if she hadn't seen the slight upturn of his lip that signaled he was kidding, she would have thought that he was trying to pick a fight.

"I wonder why," she countered. She seriously missed caffeine at this particular moment. She rubbed her back and winced a bit. She hadn't had backaches until recently. But as her belly grew, so did the back pains. "Did you already have breakfast?"

"I grabbed something."

"I'm going to grab something, too, and then I'll be back to help you. I was thinking about tackling this today. You must've read my mind."

"Close. I read your list...."

It hit her like a flash: this was Luke's way of apologizing for what had happened between them the night before. He knew how she felt about her to-do list, and he was pitching in as an apology.

It was a nice gesture, and it certainly soothed her ruffled feathers, but it didn't change the fact that she was going to talk to Luke about what had happened. He wasn't getting off the hook that easily.

She wolfed down a piece of toast, a hardboiled egg and a glass of orange juice before she headed back to the family room. Luke had opened all of the boxes, and Ranger was pouncing on a piece of tissue paper that had fallen out of one of them.

"We can't have tinsel this year." Sophia surveyed the open boxes.

"Why not?"

She nodded her head toward Ranger, who had just discovered that his tail was following him.

Understanding lit Luke's face. "Good point. No tinsel." He waved his hand over the boxes. "I can't believe the stuff my mom has held on to. Look at this."

Sophia came over and took an ornament from Luke's hand. It was a gingerbread man made out of dough and painted haphazardly with food dye. One of his legs was broken off.

"That is an official Dan creation," Luke said.

Sophia studied the ornament with a faint smile on her face. "He wasn't really an artist, was he?"

Luke actually cracked a smile on that one. It was the first time he had smiled with his teeth showing since returning from Afghanistan. The military had changed him. He had always been more serious than Daniel, but he used to smile more readily when she first met him in college.

"No. Art wasn't either one of our strongpoints."

She pointed to the missing foot. "Is this your handiwork?"

Luke looked up from unpacking the other ornaments. "That's Jordan's handiwork, not mine."

"It blows me away every time I think about your mom and dad raising five kids. Five! And two sets of twins, no less. Did your mom tell you that Jordan and Josephine are coming for Christmas? They're flying in the week before. How long has it been since you've seen your baby sisters?"

Luke thought for a minute. "It's been a while." It seemed like a lifetime ago since he had seen his twin sisters. They were the youngest of the five and sometimes they seemed like complete strangers. He loved them, of course, but most of the time he didn't get them at all.

They unpacked all of the boxes and put out a few items that were a family holiday standard: the giant Frosty the Snowman candle was positioned on the fireplace mantel, a sprig of mistletoe was hung at the threshold of the family room, and an ornately dressed Santa Claus was placed in his usual spot on the coffee table. The rest of the items were placed neatly on one side of the room. Once Luke's younger twin sisters arrived from college, they would bring in a live tree to decorate.

Sophia gave the room a final visual inspection. She wasn't surprised anymore that the two of them made a good team; she was just grateful. But because they were getting along so well, she found it hard to rock the boat and bring up what had happened the night before. She wasn't going to forget about it, but it seemed like a good idea to postpone the talk.

"Do you think your mom would let me have this?" She held up the footless gingerbread man ornament.

Luke straightened upright and squinted his eyes a bit to examine the ornament. "I don't see why not."

Sophia nodded and held the ornament in her hand; she rubbed her finger over the rough surface. She could imagine a young Daniel painting the ornament, and it made her think about her own son. One day, Danny would make a homemade ornament for her. She brought the old ornament up to her nose and breathed in.

She let her mind take a trip down melancholy lane, which was a mistake. The minute she started to think about all of the Christmases her son would have without his father, her emotions took over, and the tears started to well up in her eyes.

"What are you doing?" Luke was looking at her with a horrified expression.

Embarrassed, she swiped at the tears, which fell unchecked onto her cheeks.

"Are you crying?" Luke asked. His tone now matched the horrified expression.

"No." That was a ridiculous thing for her to say.

"Yes, you are." He took a step closer. "You're crying. Why are you crying?"

The absolute horror in his voice bordered on panic, which actually made her laugh. If she had been bleeding from her eyes, Luke could handle that without any problem. But tears? The man was like a deer caught in headlights. Now she was laughing and crying at the same time, which was a very odd thing to experience.

She laughed for a minute and then started to cry harder.

"Christ, Sophia! Stop that!" Luke reached over and grabbed something from the top of the Christmas pile and was at her side. He sat down on the couch beside her and began to roughly rub the tears from her face. He swiped the cloth over her entire face, smashed her nose down, and covered her mouth in the process. A piece of lint broke loose and was sucked into her windpipe. Caught off guard, she started to cough; she reached up and stopped Luke. She pulled the item from her face.

"Hey, hey, hey...a little rough, Captain Brand!" She glared at him accusingly before she looked down at his makeshift tissue. "What is this? What are you wiping my face with?"

"I don't know."

Sophia turned it over in her hand and saw the word *Barbara* embroidered on it. "It's your mom's Christmas stocking from when she was a kid! Your grandmother made this, Luke! It's a family heirloom! How could you use it to wipe my face!? And none too gently I might add...."

"How did I know what it was? It was available. I grabbed it."

"There's a lot of stuff available all over the place! That doesn't mean that you wipe a person's face with any of it! Especially not the stocking your grandmother *hand-stitched* for your mother! Geez!"

"The situation called for action." This was said with total seriousness.

Sophia took the tail of her shirt and dabbed it over the stocking to blot the tear-stained material. "And the stocking got in the way, is that it? A casualty of war?"

For a minute, the two of them sat on the couch together and looked from the stocking to each other. They both started to smile. "Well," she said, "that's one way to get me to stop crying. Thank God you didn't tell me to blow!"

Luke cracked a smile. "That was next."

Sophia held out the stocking in front of her. "Can you tell that I cried all over it?"

"It's fine."

"You didn't even look."

"What do you want me to look at?"

"I want you to look at the stocking. What's the matter with you? Could you focus for *one* second? Why are you being so difficult? Just look at the stupid stocking, already."

Luke looked at the stocking.

"Well?" she prompted.

"It's fine."

She sighed in exasperation and waved it at him. "Just put it back where you found it, will you? I just pray that your mother doesn't notice, but we both know that Barbara Brand notices absolutely everything! And if she does I will throw you right under the bus without any hesitation or guilt!"

Luke dropped the stocking on top of the pile. "You'd do that, wouldn't you?"

"Yes, I would."

"I always knew you had a mean streak, Soph. I always knew."

Luke sat down beside her and the mood in the room lost the humorous edge. Luke's eyes swept her face, his sharp, blue eyes concerned.

"What was that crying stuff all about, anyway?"

She let out a long breath. "Self-pity. Plain and simple. I started to think about my son and all of the Christmases we were going to have without Daniel…" She shrugged and sniffed loudly. "There are a lot of mental roads I know better than to let myself travel down, because in the end, feeling sorry for myself doesn't change anything, you know? But knowing better and actually not doing something are two entirely different things."

Luke slid his arm around her shoulder, gripped her shoulder tightly and pulled her into his body. "I'm proud of you."

Sophia found herself sinking into his hard, warm body without a second thought. She tipped her head back. "You're…proud of…me?"

"You bet."

"Why?"

"You're a tough woman and you're handling this situation like a marine…."

"Well, thank you, Captain." This was a compliment of epic proportions coming from Luke.

"Except when you're leaking all over the couch,"

Luke added as he gave her arm a squeeze. "Then, you're just another weepy dame."

She pulled back and punched him on the arm. "Thanks a lot, Brand. You know, you aren't exactly good at the 'providing comfort' thing. You almost rubbed my nose right off my face with that stocking!"

"In my own defense, I don't have a lot of practice. My men don't typically cry. But, if one of them did, I sure as hell wouldn't gently wipe away his tears."

"Hey...*gentle* is a matter of opinion."

"You're just a chick. What do you know?"

"I know if someone is trying to rub my nose right off my face, I can tell you that!"

Luke glanced over at her. "You're never going to let me live that one down, are you?"

"I doubt it," she said easily. "Hey! Perhaps you should pack some Christmas stockings in with your gear just in case one of your men has a moment."

"I'll put it in the suggestion box."

"See that you do," Sophia bantered. "Do you think I could become an honorary marine for submitting a winning suggestion like that? I could *literally* change the face of the military."

"Sergeant Sophia Brand," Luke played along.

"Ooh-rah," she said with a smile.

He tugged on her ponytail. "Ooh-rah."

They smiled at each other for a moment and then Sophia's stomach growled loudly. They both looked down at her belly.

"Lunch?" she asked.

"That works."

Sophia accepted his offered hand. "You know...I was about to go stark raving mad just before you arrived. At that point, I was glad to see any sign of human life…" She paused.

Luke filled in the rest for her. "Even me."

Sophia glanced up at him to gauge his mood and then she laughed. He was teasing the both of them. "Yes. Even you. And I wouldn't have thought it could be possible, Luke, given our rather rocky past… But I'm having a great time with you, and I'm glad that you came home early to see me." She stopped at the threshold of the room to look up at him. "I really am."

Luke met her gaze. He knew that he had to stop closing his heart to her, so he said, "I'm glad to be here with you too, Sophia. There's no place on earth I'd rather be than right here with you now."

She planted her hands on her hips. "Not even back with your men?"

"Not even back with my men."

Sophia was once again caught off guard by Luke's words. She had been teasing him, but his response had been serious.

"You keep me on my toes, Brand, that's for sure. Just when I think I have you figured out, you say something that surprises me." She smiled up at him, before she began to walk toward the kitchen.

Luke reached out and grabbed her wrist. He tugged it gently to get her to stop. She looked over her shoulder questioningly. He had a mischievous twinkle in his striking blue eyes as he glanced upward. She followed his eyes up to the sprig of mistletoe.

She felt a blush race up her neck to her cheeks. Her heart started to beat in the most ridiculous way. Did he mean to kiss her? Did she mean to let him?

She tried to make light of the situation. "What would your girlfriends, *plural,* think?" She tried to keep her tone casual, but she heard an annoying waver in her voice.

Luke quirked up his lip and his eyes radiated a heat that she had never experienced before from him. No wonder the women threw themselves at Luke. When he turned that gaze on her, she started to forget herself and felt inclined to melt into his arms.

"I'm not going to make love to you, Sophia." When he said "make love," a shiver raced right up her spine. "It's just a kiss."

"Between friends," she said on a rush of air; she wished that her heartbeat would slow down. Something odd flickered in his eyes, but it came and went before she could pin down the emotion.

"Something like that," Luke murmured as he brought her hand up to his lips. Sophia watched him press his mouth to the back of her hand.

The moment came and went quickly, and when he released her hand, she felt like a real lunatic. She couldn't believe that she actually thought Luke was going to kiss her on the mouth. Of course, he wasn't going to do that! And she was glad that he hadn't. Sort of...

That simple kiss had made her feel sensations in places throughout her body that hadn't been revved up since Daniel last touched her. It was unnerving and exciting all at the same time. She had the distinct feeling that Luke knew how to love a woman's body like nobody's business. Allie was right: Luke was a seriously sensual, sexy, handsome man.

How could she have missed that?

Why was she noticing *now?*

Chapter Eight

Several days had passed since Luke had kissed her beneath the mistletoe, and Sophia couldn't seem to stop thinking about the sensation of his lips pressed against her skin. It had been an innocent gesture that had left an indelible mark on her brain.

Of course, Luke hadn't meant anything by it. And yet… Her pulse would quicken whenever her mind replayed the moment over again. And she hated to admit it, but the moment was never far from her mind. Her brain had conjured a slow-motion image of his piercing blue eyes as he bent his head down to press his lips to her hand.

His eyes had locked on hers, drew her in and held her motionless with their intensity.

Once Luke locked his eyes on you, he had you. It was the first time she had felt the power of his gaze; it was magnetic. Animalistic. That one look had made her heart race in a way it hadn't raced in a very long time. Perhaps not ever. She felt a tingle in her stomach whenever she remembered the feel of his warm breath as it brushed across the back of her hand just before his lips made contact with her skin. The minute his lips had touched her, goose bumps had cropped up on both of her arms and she had involuntarily sucked in her breath. Even now, if she closed her eyes, she could still imagine the soft tickling sensation the stiff hair of his goatee created as it brushed past her knuckles.

And she closed her eyes often.

Reliving that innocent kiss had become somewhat of a favorite pastime. Had she conjured up all of this romantic euphoria out of boredom or grief? She couldn't be certain. All she knew was that for the past couple of days, Luke had made all of her bells and whistles go off, and she flat-out enjoyed it. Enjoyment laced with a heavy dose of guilt.

"You okay?"

Sophia opened her eyes; Luke was staring at her over his paper. They had fallen into a comfortable routine; Luke with his coffee, she with her tea. He would read the paper while she wrote out endless items on her to-do list. Luke had blended in with her daily routine seamlessly.

He seemed to fit her in a way she hadn't imagined possible. He wasn't Daniel, and yet he fit her just as well, in his own unique way.

"I'm fine," she replied quickly, irritated with herself that Luke had caught her daydreaming about that stupid kiss. And, to make matters worse, she hadn't been able to get Allie's words out of her mind. She couldn't stop herself from trying to catch Luke giving her "the look." She had caught Luke looking at her many times, but never with "the look." Most of the time the "look" he was giving her was one of curiosity, because he was probably wondering why every time he looked up, *she* was staring at *him*.

Damn Allie for sticking that ridiculous idea in her brain!

She looked back at her list and tried to shove the kiss back into the recesses of her mind. She wrote another item on the list and then stared at the words she had written.

Take Luke to Daniel's grave.

She stared at Luke and tapped her pencil on the paper while she thought. Finally, she made a decisive circle around the latest item and drew an arrow to point to the top of the list.

Luke had been home for nearly a week and he had yet to make any mention of visiting Daniel's grave. His family was due home in a day. And just as Luke thought it best that their reunion be a private event, she *knew* that it should be just the two of them present the first time Luke visited his brother's grave.

It needed to be done.

"What now?" Luke asked in an exasperated tone. He had bent the corner of the paper down and was examining her through slightly narrowed eyes.

"What do you mean?"

"I know that look; I know that tapping. Whatever's on that psychologist's mind of yours, just spit it out so I can deal with it."

He was blunt, so she was blunt.

"We need to go visit Daniel's grave."

Everything in Luke's body tensed. Sophia was watching him closely; she saw his jaw clench and the pallor of his face whiten. The long scar that ran along the edge of his jaw became more prominent. He studied her for a moment before he snapped the paper back into place and returned to his article.

She wasn't about to be deterred by him. She knew that Luke was good at intimidating people; he was a soldier first and a man second. But he didn't intimidate her. And he was going to visit Daniel's grave if she had to drag him there herself!

She had always believed in divine intervention, and she realized now that Luke was here to help her cope with Daniel's death, and in return, she was here to help him. And she intended to do just that.

"It needs to be done," she said, before she drained the rest of the tea from her cup.

He ignored her and she didn't care. She had put off her discussion with him about the nightmare he had experienced several nights before, but she couldn't put this off. It was just too important.

She stood up, rinsed out her cup at the sink before she returned to the table. She scooped up Ranger, who had been upside down on the table between them, gave him a scratch on his chops and then put him down on the ground.

"No time like the present." She stood next to Luke. He didn't bother to look at her.

Silly man! He actually was under the mistaken impression that she was going to give up!

She poked his shoulder with her finger, which got a snarl out of him but no verbal response.

She poked him again. This time he sighed heavily, dropped the paper and glared at her.

"Are you trying to pick a fight with me?" he asked, disgruntled.

Sophia crossed her arms over her chest. "Do you

want a fight?" She threw the question back at him. Her tone was razor sharp.

He leaned back a bit, his eyes still narrowed. "Maybe."

She didn't back off. "Fight all you want, Lucas. You're going to go see your brother. It needs to be done, and it's going to be done today!"

Luke picked up her list, glanced at it and then tossed it back onto the table. "Why? Because you have it written down on your damned list?"

Sophia had zero intention of budging. Luke needed to see Daniel. It needed to be real for him. And it needed to be done without a crowd.

Sophia set her jaw. "You're going, Luke. Your father gassed the truck up for me before they left, and you only need your right leg to drive. There isn't one good reason why we shouldn't go."

Luke pushed back from the table abruptly and stood up. She saw him wince slightly when he put full weight down on his left leg. "I can think of plenty," he said in a low, controlled voice.

She cocked her head to the side. His eyes were narrowed, and so were hers. "Name one."

He clamped his mouth shut and said nothing. She knew she was pushing him, that he was uncomfortable. But his discomfort would grow a thousandfold if he saw Daniel's grave for the first time with his entire family as witnesses. He needed to go now, and she wasn't going to stop until he agreed.

He'd thank her later. Most likely.

After a minute of Luke staring her down, he said in measured words, "Why do you always have to do this, Sophia? Why can't you leave well enough alone? Were we getting along too well, is that it? Too calm for you? You had to get in there and stir up the pot?"

"Don't try to put the blame on me so you can avoid this," she retorted. "I'm not doing this to pick a fight with you because I'm bored." She waved her hands when she talked. "I'm doing this to *help* you, for all the thanks I'm getting!"

He grabbed for his cane and moved away from the table. "Thanks," he said with a large dose of sarcasm.

"You're welcome," she snapped back as she followed behind him. "Let's get ready to go."

Luke stopped abruptly, spun around, and she nearly bumped into him. They were face-to-face. She had her hands on her hips; he wore a scowl.

She nodded her head toward the cane. "You know, it doesn't do a whole heck of a lot of good being held in your hand like that. It actually has to touch the ground for it to be effective."

He ignored her comment and said through gritted teeth, "I'm not going."

"Yeah," she said easily, "you are."

Luke gave her a look that she supposed was meant to stop her in her tracks. He turned back to the stairs with a frustrated growl.

At the bottom of the stairs she said, "You have to do this, Luke."

Luke paused on the third step and she waited. Finally, he turned back around. His handsome face was hard and tense. "Why are you pushing this?"

"You need to see Daniel's grave," she said simply, quietly.

"Why?

"It won't be real until you do."

Luke ran his hand over his head in a frustrated gesture. He pinned her with his bright blue eyes. "Did it ever occur to you that I don't *want* it to be real?"

"Yes."

"It occurred to you?"

"Yes! It's what I do for a living, for crying out loud."

He moved down one step. "If it occurred to you, then why are you pushing me so damn hard?"

"I'm doing this for you."

"You're doing this for me?" His eyes were blazing. "This kind of favor I can do without!"

"No, you can't!" Sophia raised her voice and waved her arm toward the door. "Do you think that I wanted to watch them bury my husband? No! I didn't! But it needed to be done. I needed to see it, Luke, so I didn't spend the rest of my days waiting for him to come walking back through that door! You have to stop pretending that he's just away, on a trip. He's not away on a trip! He's gone!"

"I know that."

"Do you?"

"Yes," he said in an oddly quiet voice.

"Do you?" she repeated more forcefully.

"Yes!"

"Have you even cried for him, Luke?"

He looked at her as if she was crazy. "I'm a marine."

"He was your twin!" she snapped back. "Marine or not, you need to say goodbye to him. You need to cry for him. Of all the stupid things we teach our boys in this country, that men don't cry is about the most idiotic!"

"What in the hell do you think it will prove? You think that if I *cry* for Dan I won't feel like someone has yanked out half my guts? It doesn't work that way, sweetheart!"

"Don't you patronize me, Lucas Brand! I'm not your

'sweetheart,' I'm your friend, and I deserve a little respect from you."

When the word *friend* came out of her mouth, Luke felt his stomach clench into a tight knot. No matter how many times he told himself to think of her that way, he couldn't. Even now, when she was ticking him off beyond belief, he wanted her. His body ached for her. Especially now, when she was riled up and her lovely face was flushed pink with emotion, and her hazel eyes had turned a dark shade of forest green.

She was everything he wanted in a woman: strong, independent, incredibly smart, and sexier now than she had ever been. She wasn't intimidated by him. She wasn't afraid to stand up to him, or call him on his crap. It was a turn-on. His hands wanted to strip her down and stroke every silken inch of her curvaceous body. That was his idea of heaven on Earth.

It took every last ounce of his willpower not to close the distance between them, mold her body into his and taste those full, tempting lips of hers. He wanted to kiss the breath right out of her. Kiss her until the word *friend* was permanently eradicated from her brain. But whenever he came close to crossing that line, Luke would look down at her belly, and that would stop him cold.

His nephew was the only thing that sobered him up and helped him keep his hands, and lips, to himself.

Sophia watched the expression in Luke's eyes as they roamed her face. She had to admit that the look he was giving her was more sensual than "friendly." He was looking at her with the same hungry expression he had given the apple pie she had baked the day before.

She shifted uncomfortably under his scrutiny. He wasn't saying a word; he just stood there and stared at her with an undeniably provocative look in his eyes. She opened her mouth to break the silence, but Luke broke the silence for her.

"You really know how to piss me off."

That shattered the tension, and she laughed out loud. Her hands went to her hips again and she smiled up at him.

"You really tick me off too, Luke."

He took another step down. "No one speaks to me the way you do."

"I know," she agreed easily.

"Then why do I let you?" he asked, his eyes never leaving hers.

She shrugged. "I'm your friend." For some reason, she felt that she needed to establish that boundary between them.

Luke's eyes took in the features of her face until they finally stopped at her mouth and lingered. She involuntarily licked her lips. His eyes traveled slowly back up to her eyes, and there was a satisfied glint in his.

"I don't have any female friends." There was a husky quality in his voice that sent a shiver right up her spine. Her heart started to thud and she felt weak in the knees.

She touched her hair nervously and wondered how he had turned the tables on her so quickly. "There's a first time for everything."

"Perhaps…" Luke said softly; she had the distinct feeling that he was saying that just to shut her up. Either way, Sophia was thrown off by the predatory look in Luke's eyes. She had never seen it before, but every nerve in her body was responding to it.

For a split second she wondered if this was "the look" Allie had mentioned, but her brain immediately rejected it.

The lengths this man would go to get out of something! It had to be that. He wasn't so hard up that he would desire a woman as pregnant as she was. She was nearly bursting at the seams and getting bigger by the minute!

She took a step back; she wanted to put a bit of space between Luke and herself. Her body was betraying her, but her mind was on task.

"Are we going, then?"

His expression shifted from predatory to amused. "You're relentless."

"Yes. I am."

He leaned back against the railing. "Why is this so important to you?"

"Why was it so important for you to come here a week early so we could work things out between us without an audience?"

"I knew it was best for you. For us."

"Exactly." She finally had him right where she wanted him. Luke never argued with logic. "I know this is best for you. For us. You need to say goodbye to Daniel without an audience. Once your family gets here, you know how your mom will react. It's not like you will be able to avoid the cemetery forever. Let's do it now."

"All right."

He conceded so easily that Sophia had to confirm it. "All right?"

"Is there an echo in here?" Luke started up the stairs. Sophia followed. So did Ranger.

"Oh, be quiet!" Sophia said playfully. "If you weren't such a stubborn pain in the rear end, we would already be halfway there!"

They parted at their doors. He saluted her. "Touché."

They threw on their winter clothes and loaded into his father's dark blue Ford truck. Sophia wrapped her arms tightly around her body and watched her breath materialize as a curl of steam in front of her face. She pulled her scarf up over her mouth and nose.

The tires crunched on the packed snow as Luke slowly drove the truck up the driveway to the main road. "It's a snow sky," he said.

Sophia nodded but didn't uncover her face. Luke glanced over at her with an amused look. He didn't seem the least bit bothered by the frigid air in the truck.

She pulled down her scarf. "I thought it was hot in Afghanistan."

"It is. But it's freezing in the mountains. This is nothing."

She pulled the scarf back over her face and waited for the heater to start working. They were halfway to the family's church before Sophia felt the heat blast into her eyes. It was right about the time her stomach started to churn with nerves. She had been so determined to get Luke to the gravesite that she hadn't considered her own feelings about seeing Daniel's grave again. His mother went to the site every week, no matter what the weather. Hank and Tyler hadn't been back since the funeral. She had made the trip a few times, but she always felt like crying when she did, so she had stopped. Until now. Until Luke. This was something that she simply had to do, tears or no tears.

Her hands started to sweat inside her gloves and she felt nauseous as they pulled into the abandoned churchyard. Most of the headstones in the small graveyard to the left of the church were covered with snow and ice. Some had been cleared by relatives.

Luke shifted the truck into Park and he leaned forward to rest his weight on the steering wheel. He looked at the headstones, his expression unreadable.

But Sophia could imagine what he was thinking. It never occurred to either one of them that Daniel would leave them so soon. Luke had tempted death for a decade, and yet his brother was the one to lose his life to war.

No doubt Luke couldn't make sense of that contradiction.

None of them could.

"No time like the present," Luke finally said and switched off the engine. He met her at her side of the truck and helped her out. "Lead the way," he said, and she complied.

They walked together slowly, arm in arm. She held on tightly to Luke's arm so she wouldn't slip. The baby, who had started to kick her furiously during the ride to the church, had suddenly quieted.

She pointed ahead. "He's down this row. At the very end. Under that tree."

The short walk seemed to take forever, until they finally reached Daniel's resting place. Luke's face was devoid of expression as he stared down at the snow-covered headstone that marked his twin's grave. He stood perfectly still, at attention; both of his hands gripped the handle of his cane as he stared at the grave.

Sophia unhooked her hand from his arm and bent down to brush the snow from the headstone.

"Careful," Luke ordered, softly.

Sophia nodded and continued with her task. She wanted Luke to see Daniel's name. She lowered herself down, used the headstone for support, before she brushed the snow from the name.

When Daniel's name was exposed, Sophia shook

her head slightly. "Hello, my dear husband…my dear friend." She pressed her fingertips to her lips and then pressed her fingers to the headstone.

She looked over her shoulder. Luke hadn't moved. She reached her hand out to him and he helped her to her feet. They stood side by side; neither of them said a word. Luke's arm came around her shoulders and he squeezed her. She leaned into him, glad for his offer of comfort and warmth.

Words didn't help. Words didn't change anything. They both knew that. But being there with Luke did make her feel better, and she could only hope that he was feeling the same way about her presence.

Finally, silently, Luke walked over to the headstone and touched it with his gloved hand. He said something under his breath that she couldn't make out before he turned back to her and nodded his head.

She knew he'd seen enough. So had she.

It was a quiet ride back to the ranch. It was a quiet walk back into the house. After they dropped their coats and boots at the front door, Luke went to the stairs while Sophia paused at the kitchen doorway.

"I'm going to take a shower," Luke said. "Are you okay?"

Sophia nodded. This was the caring side of Luke she was starting to get to know. That she was starting to love. "I'm okay."

"I'll get a fire going when I'm done."

"Sounds good," she said. "Luke?"

"Hmm?" When he turned toward her, she could suddenly see how weary he was. How his leg and Daniel's death had worn on him. She could see it because he wasn't bothering to hide it from her.

"It really is a stupid thing our society tells boys about

crying. Men should cry if they lose someone they love. I'm not going to fill little Danny's head with that nonsense. If men weren't supposed to cry, why would God give them tear ducts?"

Luke gave her a halfhearted smile. "I'll get that fire going soon."

"Okay." She had said her piece; time to let Luke work things out for himself.

In the shower, Luke pressed his hands against the wall and let the hot water run down his face. It burned and the burn felt good. What was Sophia doing to him? What was that woman doing?

She seemed to be able to see right through him. No one had ever been able to read him this well, other than Dan. Dan knew him inside and out. Now it seemed that Sophia knew him, too. The woman had pushed him right up to the edge, and then, when they had gotten home, she had booted him right over it.

He bent his head down and closed his eyes. Tears squeezed out of his eyes and blended with the steaming water from the showerhead. It felt right to cry for his brother.

It was the release he needed. And the fact that Sophia had given him permission had somehow made it possible. That woman already had his heart; now she had wormed her way right into his brain.

He loved her more now than he ever had before. Perhaps he was truly loving her for the first time; perhaps before, he had loved the woman he had thought she was, and now he was loving the woman he knew her to be.

Either way, that woman had him, heart, mind, body and soul. He was hers. She might not want him. But she had him.

Chapter Nine

She found him later in the library building the fire he had promised her. He greeted her with his version of a smile, and she could see that he was clean-shaven and refreshed. She curled up in her favorite chair and pulled the comforter over her legs. Ranger, who had been keeping her company in the kitchen, dragged himself up onto the ottoman and shared a corner of the comforter with her.

"How's it going?" she asked him as she watched him build the fire. His back was wide and the muscles rippled beneath the cotton of his T-shirt as he loaded wood into the fireplace. The man was covered in hard, thick muscle, where Daniel had been a lean runner. Both were very appealing physiques in their own way. With his back turned, her eyes roamed over his body without censure. There was something she particularly enjoyed about how the muscles bulged in his arms whenever he tensed them in the slightest way.

She also enjoyed the feel of his strong, thick arms beneath her fingers whenever she had to hold on to him for balance. In the beginning, she had spent all of her time with Luke picking out all of the details that reminded her of Daniel. Now she found that she spent most of her time noticing the little details that made Luke distinctly Luke.

Luke held on to his cane and levered himself up. He watched the fire for a moment, made certain that the flame caught, before he set himself down on the couch. Then, he answered her question.

"I've recovered from our little field trip, if that's what you're getting at."

"That's what I was getting at." There was a smile in her voice. She snuggled farther down into the chair, pulled the comforter up to her chest and sighed happily.

"I'm so glad that you showed up, Luke. These fires are the best part of my day."

He didn't respond with words, but he did give her a slight nod. That was another thing she had to become accustomed to with Luke; he was a man of few words. His actions were his words, and it had always been the exact opposite with Daniel. Daniel would talk your ear off without thinking twice. It was hard to pry a full sentence out of Luke most of the time, but she was learning to enjoy the silences between them. She was also learning to pay close attention to what Luke *did* say, because each word counted for something, and he never said anything he didn't mean. She loved that about him. As it turned out, there were many things that she loved about Luke. She loved his strength, she loved his honesty and she loved the fact that he thought of her baby as his own.

Perhaps she had always loved him, in her own way; she just hadn't realized it until Luke had come home early for her sake. That one act opened her eyes. And her heart.

"Can I ask you a question?" she broke the silence.

"Shoot."

"Have you ever thought about getting out?"

"Out of what?"

"You know…the military?"

Luke glanced over at her. He had rested his chin in the palm of his hand; his legs were stretched out in front of him. "No."

"Not once?"

"Not once," Luke said without hesitation.

She paused for a minute before she continued. "Not even after your leg?"

"No."

For some ridiculous, unknown reason, her heart sank. What did she think? That one week with her would make him quit his military career? One week with her, and he would be willing to stop putting his life in danger, come to Boston and get to know his nephew in a way that his brother would never be able to do?

Unfortunately, there was a part of her that didn't think this sounded all that unreasonable.

"Not even after Daniel?" Yes, she went there. She didn't know why she went there, but she did.

"No," Luke replied smoothly. "Not even then."

"Why not?" Her voice sounded shrill.

"The military is my life. It's the only life I know. I wouldn't know who I was without it."

"So, you're going to retire a marine?"

"That's the plan. God willing."

"Or die a marine." There was a bite in her tone.

That got his attention. His eyes were focused directly on her. "Either way, I'm going to die a marine."

"And what happened the other night doesn't bother you?"

"Nothing happened." Luke's granite expression was back in place.

"Something happened."

Luke leaned forward and rubbed the palms of his hands together. "You need to learn when to leave well enough alone with me, Soph. I'm not Dan."

"I never said you were," she said in a low, calm tone. "All I'm doing is having a conversation with a friend. Perhaps you should ask yourself why you're getting so defensive."

Luke sliced the air with his hand. "I'm not going to ask myself a damn thing when it comes to the other night."

"That's where you and Daniel are one and the same… You're both so pigheaded. There's no reasoning with either one of you! Stubborn jackasses right to the core!"

Luke sat back and crossed his arms over his chest. "Is that your professional opinion?"

Sophia felt her blood pressure skyrocket. "You might not want to hear it, but I work with men and women coming back from combat, and all of them have some sort of post-traumatic stress. I've seen it time and time again. You're tough, but you aren't immune. And being a soldier isn't everything you crack it up to be. Most of the time, the military just chews you up and spits you out when they're done. A lot of the veterans I see don't ever get the help they truly need."

Luke didn't respond for a minute, let the silence drag on. Then he said stiffly, "Are you done?"

"Yes."

"Are you sure?"

"I said yes, you royal pain in the butt!"

Sophia stopped talking and started watching the fire. She hadn't liked any of his answers, but she hadn't been a bit surprised. Any thoughts she had conjured up recently of Luke leaving the military in order to get to know her son was all a bunch of fantasizing. She had only herself to blame for the disappointment she felt. She wasn't being reasonable.

He was still staring at her, probably sizing her up, trying to figure out her angle. Finally, he restarted the conversation.

"What would you have me do? Give up my life? To do what, exactly? I'm no rancher."

She shrugged beneath the comforter. "I wasn't thinking of anything specific. I was just wondering if you thought you should give your family a break. Your mom shouldn't have to worry about losing another son."

"And what about you?" There was a gravelly quality to his voice that made her move her eyes from the fire to his face.

"What about me?"

"I thought maybe you didn't want to lose another Brand man."

Another bull's-eye. Did the man know absolutely everything that was in her head? It was unnerving!

Sophia pushed herself up a bit and met his gaze head-on. "I suppose I was talking about myself, too. More about my son, actually. You are the closest thing to Daniel he's ever going to have. It'd be nice if you didn't go off and get yourself blown up, as well."

What she had said sounded harsher in words than it had in her head, but it was the truth, and she couldn't make herself regret saying it.

To her surprise, Luke said, "I've thought about that."

"You have?"

"Quite a bit. That boy you're carrying is the closest link I have to my brother. He's my top priority, and whether you believe it or not, that's a strange concept for me. Nothing has ever taken priority over my career, and I sure as hell didn't expect it to happen now." He pinned her with his sky-blue eyes. "But it has happened, and I want little Danny to know me. I want to know him. Without my damned consent, you and your boy have changed everything!"

Quietly, she said, "I didn't know you'd given it that much thought."

"How could you unless I spelled it out? We've never been great at getting to the heart of things with each other...."

"Past tense," she added.

"I hope that's the case." Luke rubbed his hands together. "I'm trying here, Soph. I don't always do the right thing, and I sure as hell don't always say the right thing. But I *am* trying."

"I know you are, Luke. And I'm trying, too. You don't know how good it is to hear you say you want to be a big part of Danny's life. It means more to me than anything. It's a blessing."

"He's the blessing," Luke said without hesitation. "That boy—" he nodded toward her belly "—is the blessing. To me."

"It makes me feel good to hear you say that, too. Honestly, because of our past, I didn't really know how you'd feel about this baby. And, no matter what I tell other people, or what kind of brave front I put on, I'd be lying if I said that I'm not scared that I won't be able to raise Danny on my own without…"

"You're not on your own," Luke broke in. "You have me. The two of you have me. I'll help take care of Danny any way I can." He rubbed his hands together and dropped his head. "And, if you let me, I'll come to Boston and visit the two of your whenever I can."

Her words caught a bit in her throat as they came out. "I'd like that. You're welcome anytime."

Luke sat back and gave a nod. Business was conducted, and concluded, satisfactorily. "Good. I'm glad we worked that out."

She could still feel his eyes on her, and then he said, "You aren't going to start crying again, are you?"

"You're not going to let me live that down, are you? I'm pregnant, you know. I do have hormone issues!"

Luke held up his hand in quick defeat. "Hey, I was just going to offer you a box of tissues or something."

"Or a Christmas stocking, Captain?" she threw back quickly.

He winked at her. "Whatever works."

The next morning, Luke was the one to answer the phone when his family made their daily "checkup" call to Sophia. It was time to give them fair warning that he was at the ranch, and from the anxious sound in his mother's voice, he had no doubt that they would be moving up their arrival time. His family couldn't wait to welcome him home, and he was grateful. But there was a very real part of him that didn't want to deal with anyone other than Sophia. Selfishly, as much as he loved his parents and his siblings, this time alone with the woman he loved had been a dream coming true. He hated for it to end.

Once his family arrived, the dynamic between them would change. It was inevitable. The minute you threw other people into the mix, that was the result. And Luke didn't want things to change between Sophia and him. He liked things just as they were. Other than the fact that he wasn't at liberty to hug her, caress her and kiss her anytime he pleased, which would be his ultimate and impossible scenario, things couldn't be better.

But, on the flip side, having his family as a buffer might just be the very thing he needed. His desire for Sophia was escalating every day. He went to bed wanting her and he awakened wanting her. And the more receptive she was to him, the more she began to warm to him, the harder it was for him not to act on the impulse radiating from the lower half of his body.

Making love to Sophia was never far from his mind. No matter what time of the day. No matter what they were doing. He wanted to make love to her. He wanted to show her, with his body, how much he loved her.

In fact, day by day, it was becoming less of a want and more of a need. It was starting to become a worst-case scenario. Time to adapt. Time to change up the environment.

His family might just be the dose of reality he needed to get his libido under control. He was certain that having his mother fussing over him as if he was a child would kill his lust quicker than just about anything else could.

"Whatcha reading?" Sophia breezed into the kitchen looking well rested and perky. Her ponytail swung behind her as she walked and her cheeks were flushed, which gave him the impression she had already gotten in her daily yoga stretch.

He held up the baby book he had found in the library.

She gave him a bemused smile. "A little light reading, Captain?"

He didn't seem the least bit embarrassed for having been caught with the book. Instead, he pointed to something he had just read. "Says here that the baby can hear and recognize voices in the womb." He pointed at the page with his finger and looked at her. "So, Danny there will be able to recognize me once he makes an entrance."

She pulled some fruit out of the fridge. As usual, she had misjudged Luke. She would never have expected him to pick up one of her baby books. And yet, not only had she picked up, he was actually *reading* it!

"Feel free to talk to him whenever you want." She dumped some fruit into a bowl and brought it over to the table.

Before she could sit down, Luke gestured for her to walk over to where he was sitting. "Bring him over here, then." This was said gruffly, before he added, more softly, "Please."

She laughed at him and he liked the sound. "Okay."

Sophia stood directly in front of Luke and he looked up at her. "Do you mind if I put my hands on your stomach?"

She shook her head at him. "Be my guest." This was the strangest conversation she had ever had with Luke.

"I wouldn't expect this from you, Captain Brand," she said as he positioned his large, warm hands on both sides of her stomach.

"What?"

"What do you mean 'what'?" she asked incredulously. "This! You and me! You talking to my stomach." She laughed out loud again. "You have to admit that this is a bizarre scene, considering our history."

Luke held up his finger to his lips. "Shh. I'm trying to have a conversation with my nephew."

"Well, excuse me," she said with playful sarcasm. "Far be it from me to interrupt a personal conversation you're having with *my* stomach!"

Luke cleared his throat and acted as if he were about to give an important speech.

"You aren't handing down orders, you know. Just speak normally," she said as she watched him with curiosity. The marine in him was always near the surface; everything had to be planned and executed with precision.

He glanced up at her. "Are you being quiet?"

"Are you hurrying up? I'm hungry, and if you don't mind, I'd like to take my belly over to that chair and eat." She pointed at her bowl of fruit awaiting her arrival.

He drew his brows together and gave her a slightly disgruntled look, but he complied. After he had a brief conversation with his nephew, he sat back in his chair and seemed satisfied. Sophia didn't move away immediately. Instead, she reached out and put her fingers on each side of Luke's lips and lifted up the corners into a makeshift smile.

"How come you don't smile anymore? You used to smile. Remember? You used to have a nice smile before you became a marine and lost the ability to do it. Do the Marines discourage smiling, too?"

Luke gave her that "you are slightly off your rocker" look that made her smile at him broadly. She pushed up his lips up a little bit higher and said. "There. See? Doesn't that feel better?"

When she dropped her fingers, Luke's lips dropped back into their normal, unsmiling position. Sophia sat down and began to wolf down her breakfast.

He hadn't responded, so she prodded him again. "I'm serious. Your face doesn't move most of the time; it's strange. You used to smile all of the time. Now you don't. Is it against Marines protocol? Do they *frown* upon it...no pun intended."

True, she was teasing him, but she was genuinely curious about the fact that Luke had forgotten how to smile.

Luke took a sip of his coffee. "If the Marines wanted us to smile, they would have issued us one."

"Ah. I see," Sophia said before she savored her last bite of fruit. "More Marines logic. I still think you could smile once in a while when you're *not* in a combat zone. I like it when you smile. You're handsome when you smile."

Without hesitation, he said, "Then I'll smile more when I'm around you."

"Good. Start now." He was trying to please her and she was going to let him. Why shouldn't she?

"How's this?" Luke lifted up the corners of his mouth.

"Oh, my God!" Sophia shook her head. "Really bad. *Really* bad! You have to show your teeth. Okay, try again."

Luke wiped his hand over his goatee, smoothed it down, as if that would help him smile more successfully. He pulled his lips tightly over his teeth and bared them quickly.

"How was that?"

Sophia sighed dramatically and dropped her hand to the table. "You looked like you were in pain. Or crazy. Or both."

"It couldn't have been that bad." Luke crossed his arms over his chest.

Sophia nodded her head several times. "Oh. Yes, it was. Worse. I've never seen such a pathetic excuse for a smile. What have they done to you? You can't even smile properly anymore!"

Luke drained his cup and then winked at her playfully. "But I can jump out of planes and blow stuff up."

She rolled her eyes. "Fine. Good. Wonderful. You still need to remind your face muscles that they have the ability to move."

"I'll get right on it, ma'am," he said with another wink and his trademark half smile.

After breakfast they spent the rest of the morning preparing for the family to arrive the next day. Sophia was a good housekeeper who bordered on compulsive now that she was pregnant. On the other hand, Luke's mom was an *impeccable* housekeeper who knew where everything in her house belonged, right down to the last matchbook.

When the last pillow was plumped and put back into place, Sophia looked around the room with a satisfied nod. "Your mom should approve, don't you think?"

Luke leaned against the doorway to the sitting room and watched her. He had helped her right up to the last room, but now she could tell by his body language that he was done cleaning for the day. No doubt he was in the mood for an afternoon fire and a nap with Ranger.

"Mom will always find something out of place. It's just her nature."

"That's true. But I'd rather give her less to spot than

more." She looked around again. "And we have the Christmas stuff unpacked. That was a big chore."

"Relax, Soph. Mom wouldn't want you wearing yourself down on her account."

She couldn't disagree with him, and yet there was something in her that didn't want to disappoint Barbara. Barbara had always embraced her as her own from the very beginning, which only made her want to please her more. But Luke was right. She had done enough. Her back was starting to ache and she felt weary.

With one last look, Sophia gave in and walked over to where Luke was standing. She faced him and rubbed her back with a sigh.

"It's going to be strange having everyone here with us. I'm used to it just being the two of us."

"Me, too."

Her eyes snapped open wide. His bluntness surprised her. "You, too?"

"I'm not big on crowds. Not even if the crowd consists of my own family."

"Hmm."

"Your back hurting?"

She gave a self-effacing laugh. "You know what… it is. I shouldn't have been so cocky about the fact that it hasn't for most of my pregnancy."

"Perhaps you're doing too much. Maybe you need to take it easy." He was concerned about her. She heard it in his voice. She could see it in his eyes. "Come here and I'll rub it for you."

Sophia hesitated. The thought of Luke putting his hands on her again made her feel nervous; she had such a strange reaction to his touch. But the lure of a back rub won out; she moved closer to him and turned around so he could reach her back. She closed her eyes as his large hands touched her lower back; she could feel the warmth of his hands through the material of her shirt. She pressed back into his hands as his fingers found the spot that bothered her the most. She heard herself spontaneously moan with pleasure.

"I suppose I don't have to ask how that feels."

"Uh-uh." That was all she could say. She didn't want to talk; she wanted to enjoy.

Luke didn't tire quickly, and finally, she was the one to end the massage. She stepped away from him, broke the contact between them. Beneath the material of her shirt, her skin felt hot where his hands had touched her.

She turned around to face him. "Thank you. You have no idea how good that felt."

"My pleasure," he said in a soft, low tone. "Any time."

Her laugh sounded a bit nervous even to her own ears. "I may take you up on that."

After a minute she changed the subject. "You know, all of my friends worked *and* went to school when they were pregnant. All I'm doing is hanging out here at the ranch. I feel like a real wimp when my body wants to rest."

"You're too hard on yourself, Sophia. Why don't you give yourself a break? You're a good woman. I don't know too many women who would put their lives on hold in another state so their in-laws can be a part of their grandson's beginning. Maybe I don't know *any* who would do that, who would be that selfless. You're helping ease my parents' pain over losing Dan by being here, and I'm telling you, I have a lot of respect for what you're doing."

"Thank you. It just felt like the right thing to do."

"Like I said. You're a good woman. The best."

Sophia cocked her head to the side and looked up at him. "Thank you, Luke. Really. It means a lot to hear you say that. I never thought you liked me much, and I suppose I didn't think much of you in return; I'm glad those days are behind us. I owe you an apology, I think."

"You don't owe me anything."

"Yes, I do." She shifted her weight and continued to look up at him. "I misjudged you and I was wrong. You are a good man, Lucas Brand. A truly good and decent man. And for the first time I know why Daniel loved you so much, because, to be perfectly honest, I never got it. But this Luke—" she pointed at him "—is the Luke he knew. Now I know him, too."

After she finished, they both fell silent. She waited for him to reply, and she supposed he was waiting for her to continue. After a minute, she saw an amused glint enter his eyes.

"What?" she asked in response.

"Sometimes you look at me like you're looking at something under a microscope," he said, and she felt a blush of embarrassment creep up her neck. "Makes me wonder if you're trying to figure out where Dan ends and I begin."

Now he was looking at her as if *she* was something under a microscope.

She knew she was turning bright red in the cheeks, and the turn of the conversation was starting to make her feel flushed all over. There was something in Luke's eyes that made her feel like a desirable woman instead of a woman about to give birth. He was looking at her as if she was a woman worth wanting, and she just couldn't deny it anymore. Luke found her attractive. And, whether she thought it was appropriate or not, her body was responding to him. All he had to do was sweep her up in that predatory gaze of his and she would start to tingle all over.

Sophia licked her lips and thought about taking a step back from him, but her feet refused to move. Finally, she said, "You're right. I can't deny it. In the beginning, I did try to figure out where Daniel ended and you began. I think it was only natural for me to do that. But now… there isn't anything to figure out. When I look at you, Luke, I don't see Daniel anymore…I only see you."

Something primitive flashed in his eyes; something primitive in her nervous system exploded. She should have moved away, but she didn't. Instead, Luke pushed away from the wall to close the distance between them.

"I'm glad to hear it," he said in that low, gravelly voice of his that sent her pulse racing.

His hands moved to her face; his fingers pushed the tendrils that had escaped from her ponytail away from her forehead. The minute he touched her, the blood started rushing through her veins, and her breathing suddenly felt shallow; she took a sudden deep breath in through her nose. Every fiber in her body wanted to have Luke continue. Every thought in her head was screaming for him to stop.

"What are you doing, Luke?" she heard herself ask in a husky voice that didn't seem to belong to her.

"You're standing under the mistletoe."

She let out a nervous laugh. Truth be told, he was making her feel a bit giddy. "Do you want to kiss my hand again? Is that it?" It was a feeble attempt to put a humorous spin on the uncomfortable situation she found herself in.

"No," Luke said as he gently titled her chin up so he could look directly into her eyes. "I don't."

"What are you doing, Luke?" she asked again, this

time more urgently. One of them had to stop, and for some reason that person wasn't her.

"I'm going to kiss you, Sophia." Her name rolled off his tongue like a caress.

Her heart skipped a beat and she felt herself lean toward him against her brain's explicit instructions. "Do you think that's a good idea?"

His lips hovered just above hers. "No," he said huskily, "I don't."

She was about to continue the conversation when she heard the slam of a car door. It gave her the out she needed, and she took it. "Did you hear that?"

"Yes." He didn't budge.

She made an irritated sound and pushed on his chest before she stepped around him. She walked over to the window and looked outside.

"Your mom said that they'd be back tomorrow, right?"

Luke had returned to his spot in the doorway. He seemed irritatingly relaxed as he leaned against the doorjamb, while she felt like a scrambled egg.

"That was the plan." Luke didn't seem the least bit distracted by the interruption. He was watching her in an observatory fashion, as if she were some fascinating animal at the zoo. His nonchalance really ticked her off.

Her voice became shrill as she threw her hands up into the air. "Then *why* are they in the driveway right now?"

Chapter Ten

Sophia glared at Luke in accusation. "Did you know about this?"

Luke shook his head. "Apparently Mom couldn't wait to welcome me home."

Sophia peered out the window one more time before she threw up her hands. "Well, a *little* warning would have been nice."

It was out of character for her to be flustered. She didn't like the feeling. And the fact that Luke seemed completely undisturbed by this sudden change in plans served only to irritate her more.

"Look at me!" Sophia waved her hands in front of herself. "I'm a mess!"

"You look fine," he said in a slightly dismissive tone that sparked off her temper.

She snapped at him. "What do you know?"

"I think I can tell if you look okay or not. I have

eyeballs in my head," Luke replied. "Why are you getting hysterical?"

Hands on her hips, Sophia stopped in front of him. "I am *not* getting hysterical!"

Luke raised one eyebrow. "You're a little hysterical."

"Oh, zip it, Brand!" Sophia snapped. She struck the palm of her left hand with her right hand in a slicing motion to emphasize her words. "I like order. I like a plan. Your family was supposed to be here tomorrow! And now that they're here early…"

"You're hysterical," Luke broke in.

"I am *not!* And even if I am *a little*…you're one to talk, Mister Marine, who has to have everything in perfect order and perfectly planned!"

"I was trained to adapt to any situation," he said seriously. "This one included."

At this moment, she really did wish that looks could kill. Luke was having an awfully good time at her expense, and if he hadn't tried to kiss her just a minute before, she wouldn't be feeling so wigged out.

"If you so much as say one more pro-Marine thing, I'm going to personally wring your neck!"

Her threat had the exact opposite effect on Luke that she wanted. His mouth curled up into his half smile and he had the audacity to wink at her. "Ooh-rah."

Sophia balled up her fists and let out a frustrated noise.

"That's it! We're not speaking!" Luke was incorrigible, and there was absolutely nothing she could do about it. When she realized that she wasn't going to convince Luke to join her emotional unraveling, *and* that her emotional unraveling was giving him a platform to irritate her more, she quit the conversation.

Unfortunately, she was never successful at the silent treatment. So, it lasted for about thirty seconds.

"It's your fault I'm freaking out, anyway!" Sophia stomped over to a mirror in the hallway.

"I thought you weren't speaking to me...."

Sophia leaned into the mirror and examined her face. There were smudges of dirt on her forehead and on her cheek. Perfect!

"God, you are *annoying!* You just couldn't leave well enough alone, could you?"

"Hey, I'm just standing here minding my own business." He had the gall to sound genuinely innocent of any wrongdoing.

Sophia took one look at her haphazard ponytail and threw up her hands again. There was no covering up the fact that it needed to be washed. She looked a mess. And she looked guilty! That was the real problem.

"Do you call trying to kiss me minding your own business?" she hissed at him under her breath; she didn't want anyone to hear her from the other side of the door. "Why would you *do* that? What were you thinking?"

Luke actually smiled with his teeth. "I was thinking that I wanted to kiss you." He was really enjoying this. His enjoyment served only to send her frustration shooting through the roof.

With one last disgruntled look at her own reflection, Sophia spun away from the mirror and returned to her spot in front of him. "Well, you shouldn't have!"

"Probably not," he agreed easily. Too damned easily! "Is that why you're coming unhinged? It wasn't a big deal. You gotta calm down. You look like you're breaking out in hives." He gestured to her neck.

"Not a big deal?" she asked, incredulously. "*Not* a big deal!"

"Nothing happened."

"Thanks to me!" she pointed out as she narrowed her eyes at him. "You know, it's really helpful that you've picked *this moment* to say more than two sentences in a row to me after a decade of one-liners!"

"Glad to be of assistance."

"I was being sarcastic!" She heard how shrill her own voice sounded to her ears; she immediately closed her eyes and took in a sharp, soothing, calming breath.

In her mind she repeated the phrase "I am calm, I am at peace."

"What are you doing?" Luke's annoying voice punctured her mental mantra and rendered the phrase useless.

Through gritted teeth, she said, "I'm calming myself by using a meditative phrase."

A few seconds later, Luke replied, "You might want to try something else. The blotches are still there."

Sophia opened her eyes and swiveled her head toward the object of her irritation. "Blotches? I should have a big red A stamped on my belly, thanks to you! How's that for a blotch!"

With one last hateful look at Luke and his stupid, smug, handsome face, Sophia plastered a welcoming smile onto her own face, walked over to the door and pulled it open.

She was greeted at the door by a cold blast of air and the family's German shepherd, Elsa. The minute Elsa spotted Luke, she raced into the entryway.

"Hey, girl!" Luke patted his chest for Elsa to put her paws on his shoulders. When she complied, Luke roughed up the fur on her neck and back.

At the moment, Sophia wanted to strangle Luke, but

when she watched him with Elsa, it reminded her that he wasn't *completely* rotten to the core.

"Sophia, my dear! Hello!" Barbara Brand breezed into the foyer with her husband, Hank, following closely behind.

"Could you grab this, dear?" Barbara said to her tall, lean, silver-haired husband. She slipped out of her full-length faux-fur coat and handed it to Hank. As soon as Barbara was free of her winter trappings, she wrapped Sophia into her arms. "I've been so worried about you, my darling. How is my grandson?"

"We're both doing well. I'm glad to see you."

For a moment Barbara admired her with Luke's same clear, bright blue eyes. No matter what the weather, Barbara always looked as if she had stepped out of a fashion magazine; her blond hair was smoothed back into a flawless chignon and her ears were adorned with her signature pearl drop earrings. She had followed her husband to Montana, but she never let go of her Chicago roots.

Barbara pressed a kiss to Sophia's cheek before she turned her attention to her son. She moved quickly to Luke's side. She reached up and put her hands on both sides of his face. "Lucas. Lucas. You're finally home." Then, she wrapped her arms around her son and hugged him tightly.

Sophia watched as Luke engulfed his mother in a bear hug. "Hi, Mom."

When Barbara pulled back slightly to get a better look at her boy, she said, "You're so thin, Lucas. My goodness! Why are you so thin?" Then Barb reached up and touched Luke's goatee. "And this isn't my favorite!"

"He looks good, Barb! Leave the boy be." Hank slapped Luke on the back and clasped his hand with his.

"Good to see you, Dad."

"How's the leg, son?" Hank asked in his gruff, bass voice.

"Yes. How is your leg?" Barbara stepped back a bit and looked down.

"It's getting better. Don't worry."

Barbara gave him a stern look. "I'll be the judge of whether or not I should worry." She looked at her husband. "Imagine your son telling me what to do in my own house!"

For the first time in a long time, Sophia saw Luke look sheepish. His mom could put him in his place quicker than anyone she had ever seen. Luke went from surly soldier to compliant son when Barbara was around.

Barbara didn't make a move to let Luke go. She looked over at Sophia. "He hasn't been giving you too hard of a time, has he?"

Sophia and Luke locked eyes for a brief second. She shook her head. "No. He's been on his best behavior."

Until just before you arrived.

"Shame on you for not telling me you were coming home early!" Barbara said to her son.

"I wanted to surprise you," Luke said easily.

Before she could retort, Tyler, six foot four like his father and heartthrob handsome, walked through the door with the bags. "Hey! There he is!" he said as he dropped the bags on the floor and shut the door with his foot. He walked through to the entryway and engulfed both his mother and brother in a giant bear hug.

"Good to see you, man!" Luke looked genuinely happy to see his younger brother.

Tyler slapped his brother on the back several times

before he swept Sophia up into a bone-crushing hug. "Hey, sis! Miss me?"

"You have no idea." Sophia laughed. Tyler was so handsome, with an easygoing cowboy charm, that it was hard for anyone to dislike him.

"Hank, what is she *doing* in there? Do you hear hissing…?" Barbara asked in an irritated tone. Elsa was whining excitedly in the kitchen.

Sophia and Luke looked at each other, and knew exactly what was occurring in the kitchen. Elsa had found Ranger, and Ranger had decided he did not *like* being found by the German shepherd.

Barbara stopped talking and walked decisively over to the kitchen doorway. She looked in for a moment, analyzed the situation and then turned her gaze to Luke.

"Lucas, darling?"

"Yes, Mother?"

"Why is there a kitten in the kitchen?"

Hank walked over to stand next to his wife. He seemed perplexed. "There's a kitten in the kitchen, Barb."

"I see that," she replied to her husband, and then she readdressed Luke. "There's a kitten in the kitchen, Lucas. Why is there a kitten in the kitchen, Lucas?"

"That's Ranger," Luke said nonchalantly; he winked at his brother.

"Why is *Ranger* on my kitchen table?" Barbara asked in a steady, precise voice.

Hank was shaking his head. "Why is there a kitten in the house? That's what I'd like to know. There wasn't a kitten here when I left two weeks ago, and there shouldn't be one here now!"

Sophia chimed in. "It's my fault he's on the table, Barb. I'll get him off."

Sophia moved toward the kitchen, but Tyler had already threaded his way past his mom and dad to scoop Ranger up; he held him in the air to get a good look at him. "Hey, Ranger! You're a funny-looking little cat, aren't you?" He held Ranger to his chest. "Who does he belong to?"

"Us," Luke said simply.

"He's going to grow into those ears." Sophia defended Ranger.

"Of course he will," Tyler agreed easily.

"Well." Hank said, "he's going to have to grow into them somewhere else."

That sparked off a loud, boisterous debate amongst the family. Barbara and Hank lead the charge for Ranger to find a new home, and Sophia, Tyler and Luke defended the gangly kitten's right to stay at Bent Tree.

"There isn't another place. This is it," Luke reasserted. He wasn't backing down. He was determined that Ranger was going to make his home at the ranch.

"Oh, for heaven's sake, Lucas! You know that we have so many other responsibilities to attend to. What possessed you to do such a thing?" Barbara asked, but her eyes softened when she looked at Ranger tucked into the crook of Tyler's arm.

"He's just one kitten, Mom," Luke said.

Hank shrugged out of his coat and pointed his finger at his son. "That kitten needs to find another place to call his own, Luke. You tell Bill to come back over and get him. Now, that's all there is to it."

Hank gave his wife one last look before he disappeared into the sanctuary of his study.

"Are you really going to throw an orphaned kitten out into the snow at Christmas, Ma? Is that the spirit of the season?" Tyler asked before he winked at Sophia.

All of them knew that Ranger was staying. Even Hank knew it. The Brand family had never turned their backs on a stray, and they weren't about to start with Ranger.

Barbara shook her head with a heavy sigh. It was a sound that signaled to Sophia that her mother-in-law had given in without much of a fight. Barbara walked over to Tyler, took the kitten into her hands and looked into his eyes. "And where did Billy happen to find you?"

"Truck stop bathroom," Luke filled in.

Barbara made a displeased noise. "Who would do such a thing? He's just a baby."

"He's a baby who needs a home," Luke added.

Barbara eyed her son over Ranger's head for a moment. "The battle is already won, Lucas. Anything at this point would simply be a waste of artillery. Haven't those Marines taught you anything?" Barbara ended her sentence with a raised eyebrow at Luke before she turned her attention back to the kitten that had melted in her hands. "Oh, for heaven's sake…" she said again, with another shake of the head. "I suppose Ranger will do."

Luke gave Sophia a satisfied look. Barbara was hooked and Ranger had a home. It was as simple as that.

The family had gathered for a celebratory dinner in Luke's honor. Barbara planned the menu and Sophia was happy to pitch in. She was grateful for the company and the distraction. She still couldn't believe what had just happened to her. She couldn't believe that Luke had tried to kiss her; and more important, she couldn't believe that she had actually considered *letting* him kiss her!

This *must* be a rebound reaction. It had to be! There

was simply no other explanation for her behavior. Yes, she had discovered a very lovable, nurturing side of Luke she hadn't even seen before. And yes, she was enjoying his company. And yes, her body was responding to him in ways that could not be considered platonic. But, and this was a very big but, that didn't mean that she wanted anything more than friendship with Luke. And certainly, he didn't want anything more from her! The man had spent the better part of a decade giving her a stony expression and a hard time. And that was when he wasn't outright avoiding her!

Obviously the two of them were turning toward each other for comfort because they had both lost Daniel. It made sense. And it had to stop.

That's why, after she had gotten over her obsessive-compulsive meltdown, she was very glad that Luke's family had arrived when they did. Just in the nick of time!

After the dinner mess had been cleaned away, the family dispersed. Sophia, who hadn't been able to keep from seeking Luke out with her eyes all night, had been internally champing at the bit until the evening had ended and she could have a minute alone with him to set things straight. She was determined to find out what had happened between them, and to make certain that it never happened again.

Of course, whenever she had sneaked a glance at him, he wasn't looking back at her. In fact, he seemed completely relaxed and unaffected by their brief encounter. No doubt it had been meaningless to him, with his "woman in every port" attitude. No doubt he was just missing out on some random female companionship after a tour of duty, and she just happened to be convenient.

Whatever the reason, whatever the motivation, she was going to make certain it didn't happen again.

Sophia made it back to her room before Luke and claimed the bathroom first. She scrubbed the day's dirt off her body and face. Then she twisted her long wet hair up into a towel before she slathered moisturizing cream on her face.

For a minute she looked down at her belly. She was getting more pregnant by the day. She had a checkup this coming week, and she was starting to feel very impatient to have the pregnancy over so she could start getting to know her son. She also wanted to get back to her life in Boston. Whenever she emailed or spoke with her friends on the phone, she felt horribly homesick. She wanted to go home.

After she had finished her nightly routine, Sophia sat in a rocking chair next to the crib and scrolled through her emails. She was just wrapping up her responses when she heard Luke enter his room next door. She clicked on the send button, logged off and closed the laptop, then stood and pulled the towel off her head. On her way to Luke's room she dropped the towel over the tub, then ran a comb through her wet hair. Finally, with one last look in the mirror, she took a deep breath and tapped lightly on the door.

"Yeah?" Luke responded to the knock.

"You decent?" Sophia asked through the door in a hushed voice. Now that the rest of the family was milling around in the old farmhouse, she was going to have to watch the volume of her voice.

"Not likely," Sophia heard him say as he pulled the door open. His eyes gave her a clinical once-over that set her teeth on edge, before he turned back to hanging up his shirt.

She took one step inside the room and leaned her back against the wall. She watched him while he finished his chore. He was stripped bare to the waist and the top button of his jeans was undone. In spite of herself, she just couldn't stop admiring the way Luke's muscles rippled as he hung up his shirt.

Luke shut the closet door. "What's up?"

His face looked different. It took her a minute to figure out why. "You shaved your goatee."

Luke propped himself against the end of the bed. He reached up and rubbed his hand over his freshly shaven face. "No sense lighting Mom's fuse over nothing."

Sophia nodded. After a moment of uncomfortable silence, she found another way to avoid getting to the point.

"You aren't using your cane as much as you should," she replied, suddenly hesitant to start the discussion she knew they needed to have.

"Is that what you came in here to say?" he asked her. He was looking at her in a very odd way. He looked relaxed enough, but something in her gut told her that Luke was wound up tight as a drum beneath his nonchalant exterior. It was if he was waiting for something unpleasant to happen.

"No." Sophia didn't like the pouty quality to her voice, so she cleared her throat and started again. "No. It's not. But you should be using it anyway."

Luke crossed his arms over his chest and didn't bother to button his jeans. "I'll keep it in mind. Anything else?"

She didn't like his dismissive tone. "Yes, as a matter of fact, there is."

Instead of answering her verbally, he waved his fingers at her, as if to say, "Bring it on."

He was being rude, dismissive. She didn't like it. Sophia pushed away from the wall and closed the door to the bathroom behind her. She stepped closer to him and said in a low, demanding tone, "I think I deserve an explanation."

"For what?"

Now they were face-to-face. His arms were crossed over his chest; her hands were on her hips. "Are you serious?"

"You bet." He didn't bother to keep his voice down.

She waved her hand. "Shhhh."

"No one can hear us."

"You don't know that!"

Luke pulled the conversation back on track. "What's up, Sophia? What's on your mind?"

"The kiss," Sophia said bluntly.

Luke's eyes narrowed and he moved away from her. He put some distance between them before he turned back to her. "Jesus, Sophia. You're relentless. Once again you just can't leave well enough alone. Why do you have to go over and over the same issue again and again? We've already discussed this. It's over. Let it go."

"Don't put this off on me, Lucas. You tried to *kiss* me and you expect me to just forget about it?"

"Yeah. I do. Nothing happened." Luke jammed his hands into his pockets. "And my name is Luke. Not Lucas."

"I want to know why you tried to kiss me, *Lucas*. And don't try to put this off on me, implying that I'm a crazy pregnant woman! You owe me an explanation. After a decade of barely tolerating me, ignoring me and avoiding me, you try to *kiss* me? And if you don't want me to give you the third degree about something, then don't do it in the first place! I'm not one of your bimbos you can use up and toss aside like garbage. Now, explain it to me as if I'm stupid, because I really don't get it. What in the *hell* were you thinking?"

Chapter Eleven

Without a word, Luke stepped around her and jerked open the door to the bathroom. The look he gave let her know, in no uncertain terms, that he was finished with the conversation.

But she certainly wasn't. She turned slowly to face him and didn't move from her spot.

She shook her head. "Nice try. But I'm not leaving."

Luke shrugged nonchalantly and walked over to the bed with only a slight limp. His leg was noticeably stronger.

"Suit yourself," he said smoothly.

"What do you think you're doing?" Sophia asked as she watched him reach for the zipper of his worn jeans.

He pinned her with his ice-blue eyes, and she could have sworn that she detected a taunting glint in them.

"What does it look like I'm doing?" His tone was unmistakably suggestive. As those words came out of his mouth, he unzipped his pants in one quick, fluid motion.

"It looks like you're taking off your pants," she responded robotically. She knew she should admit defeat and return to her room, but she couldn't seem to move her feet.

"Your powers of observation are impressive." He said this while his pants were dropping to the ground. Luke stepped out of his pants and stood before her without any sign of modesty. He was trying to get her to leave by embarrassing her, but it wasn't going to work.

"I want an answer, Luke. Are you going to give me one?" She tried. She really did. But she couldn't take her eyes off him. She was a woman, and he was a man to be admired; she was tempted to run her hands over his skin, just to feel the strong muscles underneath. He was rock-solid and incredibly appealing.

She forced herself to jerk her eyes away from his taut abs just as he jerked the blanket back and climbed into his bed. He stopped briefly and stared her down; unsmiling, silent, he slipped onto his back. He sighed deeply as his head sank into the pillow. She watched as he pulled the blanket up to his waist and closed his eyes. She was actually glad for his closed eyes; her face felt as if it were burning up from embarrassment and...

Desire. There was no mistaking it. Her body was tingling all over; her heart was beating hard in her chest. There went those bells and whistles again, ringing loud and clear!

The room was silent for several moments while she pulled herself together. Sophia stared at Luke sprawled out in his bed and felt completely frustrated and inept to deal with him. Daniel and Luke were nothing alike when it came to stuff like this. Daniel would never do this sort of thing, and she had to admit that when it came to handling Luke, she was failing miserably.

"Oh, my *God,*" Sophia finally blurted out as she moved from her spot to stand next to the bed. She could tell by his deeper breathing that he was about to fall asleep with her standing in the middle of his room! "You are unbelievable! Truly unbelievable. Why do I even bother trying to talk to you about anything?"

Luke didn't bother to open his eyes. "If you stay in my room much longer, Sophia, I might just start to think you want me to pick up where I left off under the mistletoe...."

It took a minute for his words to sink in, but when they did, Sophia was overrun with guilt and embarrassment. The words hit too close to home. She opened her mouth and then shut it. She opened it again and then shut it again. She couldn't think of the perfect retort fast enough, and it was really ticking her off that she was standing in the middle of Luke's room acting like a beached guppy.

Finally she said through gritted teeth, "Go to hell, Luke."

She turned, walked into the bathroom and firmly shut the door behind her.

It was easy to avoid Luke for the next couple of days, and Sophia was glad, for the most part, that they could take a break from each other. There was so much to do in preparation for the holidays, and most of it required her to fill her time helping Barbara. Luke spent most of his time in the barn with his brother and father, which made keeping him at a distance an easy thing to do. There seemed to be a silent agreement of avoidance between them at this point, and even though she had zero desire to speak to him after his rude behavior, it irked her no end that Luke had decided to avoid her, as well.

And, truth be told, she missed his insufferable company. She actually felt a sense of loss without him near. She didn't understand how she could have allowed herself to get attached to him so quickly. But it made her believe that this sudden break was a good idea. After all, he was going back to active duty as soon as he was healed. He was a military man and nothing was going to change that fact. Certainly not her and her baby, no matter how much he cared for her son. Luke was Luke, and the Marines always came first.

But she couldn't stop herself from missing the jerk no matter how hard she tried, and it was that feeling of missing him that drove her to cross the threshold into his bedroom on the third morning of their unspoken pact to give each other space. He was long gone; she had heard him leave near the crack of dawn to go into town with his brother to pick up Jordan and Josephine. She walked over to the bed, picked up his pillow, and brought it up to her nose. She breathed in deeply. It smelled like Luke. She couldn't remember why his scent had ever reminded her of Daniel. He had his own very distinctive scent that seemed to drive her senses crazy.

Sophia hugged the pillow to her chest and walked over to the uniform hung on the outside of the closet. She ran her hand over the stripes on the sleeves and the rows of medals pinned to the breast. As her fingers touched each individual medal, a very disturbing thought passed through her mind: *Am I falling for Luke?*

"Am I?" Sophia asked softly, out loud. She hugged the pillow tighter to her chest for a minute, stared at the uniform for several seconds, before she threw the pillow back onto the bed.

"I could be falling for Luke," she said to herself as she returned to her room. When you stand in a man's room smelling his pillow and touching his clothing, you're either falling in love or you are a stalker.

How in the world could this have happened? Was she that weak? That hard up? That susceptible? The last thing she should be doing is developing feelings for Luke.

"Pathetic," Sophia said to herself as she slumped into her rocking chair. It took a full hour, but Sophia tired of her own self-pity and headed downstairs. Barb was busy in the kitchen preparing for her daughters' arrival home, and Hank was in his study with Ranger, his new faithful companion.

"I was wondering when you were going to show up," Barb greeted her. "Here, have some juice."

Sophia sat down at the table and gratefully accepted a tall glass of orange juice. "What time do you expect them back?"

Barb popped some bread into the toaster. "Two more hours. It's going to seem like twenty." Barb smiled at Sophia as she opened the fridge. "What kind of jam? Grape, strawberry...?"

"Do we have raspberry in there? I can't remember."

Barb pulled out a jar. "Raspberry it is."

Sophia slowly ate the toast and polished off her juice while Barb peeled a bowl of potatoes. "Can I help you with something?"

"I can always use an extra set of hands," Barb said with a smile. She put down her peeler and wiped off her hands with a dish towel. "But first, I found something you may be interested in."

"What's that?"

"Follow me and I'll show you."

They moved into the family room and Barb pointed

to a book box on the coffee table. "I found this last night in the attic. I couldn't believe I had overlooked it."

"What is it?"

"Some things Daniel saved from college."

Sophia's eyes widened. "You're kidding?"

Sophia sat down and pulled the box toward her.

"I'll give you some time to go through it."

"Thanks," Sophia said off-handedly as Barb disappeared. Her focus was completely on the box. It was like finding a hidden treasure.

Sophia slowly opened each flap of the box, pushed them down and ran her hand over the rough cardboard. She had no idea what was in the box, or how it would make her feel to explore the objects treasured enough by her husband to save them.

Carefully, and with reverence, Sophia pulled the items out of the box. Most of the items were standard and expected: his trophy from his favorite swim meet, an A paper from a political science class, an unframed picture of the two of them at their first college dance, and plastic gold beads from their trip to New Orleans Mardi Gras. He also had items in the box that didn't make any sense at all. There was a large gold paper clip, a broken fountain pen and a black marble.

Sophia spread the items out on the table and looked them over. It was strange to see her husband's college years reduced to a few random items. She would give anything to ask him what in the world possessed him to save a paper clip and a black marble. After a while, Sophia pulled the box toward her and tipped it on its side so she could load the items back into the box. At the very bottom of the box, Sophia noticed a weathered white envelope. She reached in and grabbed it. She pushed the box back to the middle of the table as she looked at the return address on the envelope.

"Second Lieutenant Lucas Brand," Sophia read aloud. The postmark was dated the year of her engagement to Daniel.

Why would Daniel hold on to this letter for so long?

Sophia peeked inside the envelope and eyed the single handwritten note. She carefully pulled the letter from the envelope and unfolded it slowly. After she read the first couple of words, her heart began to thud harder in her chest, and she felt chilled all over her body.

Dan,
Mom tells me you're engaged. Congratulations. I wish you had told me yourself, but I guess you were waiting for the right time. I want you to know that I'm really happy for you. You know me well enough to know that if I say it, I mean it. The last thing I want is for this to come between us. Nothing has ever come between us; I'm not going to let anything start now. You're my twin brother and that comes first with me. The fact that I'm in love with Sophia doesn't change the fact that I want my brother to be happy. She makes you happy, and I'm happy for you. I can't help how I feel about her any more than you can. It is what it is. I love her, but if I can't have her, then I'm at least glad that she's with a man who will take good care of her. You want me at the wedding as your best man, and I'll be there if I can get leave. I'd do anything for you, brother…even marry you off to the woman I'm in love with. I have one stipulation as your best man: never tell Sophia how I feel about her. Take it to your grave. I'll

have your word on this. I love you and I'll see
you soon if I can....

The letter continued, but Sophia stopped reading.
She sat in stunned silence and tried to make sense of
what she had just read. In his own handwriting, in his
own words, Luke had written that he was in love with
her. Suddenly everything she had been feeling from him
over the past couple of weeks became crystal clear: the
attempted kiss, the smoldering look in his eyes when
he looked at her and the very fact that he came home
early out of concern for her. As it turned out, Allie and
her instincts had been dead-on accurate. Luke loved
her. For all of these years, since they were in college,
he had loved her. And Daniel had kept his secret. How
could he have kept that from her for their entire marriage? Twin or not, he wasn't supposed to keep secrets
like that from her! What else didn't she know?

With the letter in hand, Sophia went to the kitchen.

"Anything interesting in that box?" Barb asked over
her shoulder. "My boy was such a pack rat. No telling
what junk he thought was essential to save."

Sophia held up the letter. "I found this."

"What is it, darling?"

"A letter that Luke wrote to Daniel."

"Really? Anything sordid I should know about?"
Barb joked, but when she turned her attention from the
stove to Sophia, her expression changed from humor to
concern. "What's wrong, honey? You look pale. Here,
sit down."

"I don't want to sit down, Barb. I want you to read
this."

Barb took the letter with a furrowed brow. Barb

quickly scanned the letter, but her face lacked the surprise that Sophia expected.

Without a word Barb refolded the letter, put it back in the envelope and handed it to Sophia.

"Well?" Sophia prompted.

"Come here, darling. Let's sit down. There's no sense in you getting yourself all upset. It's not healthy for the baby."

Sophia's mouth dropped open. "Don't get upset? Are you kidding? You did *read* it, didn't you?"

"Yes." Barb slid a chair back and patted it. "Here, honey. Sit down and we'll sort this out."

Reluctantly Sophia sat down at the table. Once Barb was seated, Sophia said, "Why do I get the feeling that you aren't surprised by what's in that letter?"

"Here, have a cookie. It will make you feel better." Barb offered her a plate of chocolate chip cookies that had just come out of the oven.

"No. Thank you." Sophia couldn't imagine ever feeling hungry again. Her stomach was tied up tightly into knots. A cookie certainly wasn't going to make anything better.

"To answer your question, no, I'm not surprised by the content of that letter."

"You're not?"

"No."

Sophia took a minute to digest the response. Then she asked, "So you're telling me that you knew that Luke is in love with me? Or, at least he *was* in love with me back in college?"

"Yes." This simple response sliced through Sophia's chest.

"How do you know?"

"Luke told me," Barb said simply, as if she were reading off a recipe.

"Luke told you," Sophia repeated dumbly. After a second anger bubbled up inside her and was reflected in her voice. "Who else in the family knows about this?"

"There just isn't any need to get so upset...."

"Barb, I don't want to be rude to you, but please don't tell me how to feel right now. I already had my fair share of emotional minutiae to work through when Daniel was killed and I found out I was pregnant. I honestly don't need this on top of everything else. Could you please just tell me, who else knows about Luke being in love with me when we were in college?"

"I don't believe that the past tense is appropriate. I believe that he is still very much in love with you."

Sophia could feel her skin flush bright red on her cheeks. She ignored Barb's last comment and stuck to the original question. "Who else knows?"

"Directly?"

"Directly, indirectly, through osmosis..."

"Hank knows, of course.

"Because you told him..."

"Because I told him."

"Who else?" Sophia demanded. Her stomach started to ache.

After a few long seconds, Barb said, "I suppose everyone knows in their own way. We're a tight-knit family." This was said with pride. "Secrets have a way of working their way out into the open. But none of the siblings have been told directly, to answer your question." She paused for a second before she added, "Not that anyone would need to be told. When Luke looks at you, it's there in his eyes for anyone to see."

"So what you're telling me is that I'm the *only one*

in the entire family who *didn't know* that Luke was in love with me?" Sophia quieted her voice and shook her head. "How is that possible?"

"You didn't know because you didn't *want* to know, dear, which is perfectly understandable. You were in love with Daniel...."

"Still am," Sophia broke in.

Barb gave a quick nod as she continued. "But in your heart, if you look back, you've always known on some level. You're a smart cookie." She reached out and gave Sophia's arm a pat. "I'm going to make some tea."

"I don't want any."

"Of course you do." Barb stood in front of her cabinets. "Now, where did I move the tea bags?"

"Second cabinet on the left. Behind the spices." Even to Sophia's own ears, her voice sounded robotic. She felt numb all over, as if her limbs had turned to lead. In one moment her reality had been altered; the sky was green, the grass was blue.

Sophia watched as Barb put on the kettle. She sat perfectly still, but her mind was racing. Her previous encounters with Luke were rolling through her mind like a motion picture. She tried to remember every look, everything he had ever said to her. As hard as she tried to conjure up a memory that would have given her some inkling that Luke was in love with her, all she could remember was his surly attitude, and his constant disapproval of her.

Barb placed a steaming cup of tea in front of her. "Lemon?"

Sophia shook her head.

"Honey?" Barb asked.

Another quick shake of her head. "No. Thank you."

Barb rejoined her at the table with her own cup of tea.

"I can't seem to make any sense of this, Barb." Sophia ignored the tea. "Luke has always disliked me. *Always*."

"No. He has never disliked you. He could never dislike you. He's pushed you away. For a good reason. For his own sanity. For his relationship with his brother. What better reason is there? Can you think of one?"

"Are you saying that Luke has been giving me a hard time for a decade because he's in love with me?"

"Yes," Barb said simply. "That's exactly what I'm saying."

Sophia and Barb stared at each other and for several moments neither said a word. In that brief moment of silence Sophia was able to read the sincerity in Barb's eyes. This wasn't a joke. Barb had just confirmed the content of the letter.

Sophia shrugged her shoulders with a sense of helplessness. Her entire insides were shaking, her armpits were sweating and she felt as if she wanted to scream, but instead she asked, "What am I supposed to do with all of this?"

"That depends."

"On what?"

Barb pinned her with those bright blue eyes of hers. "On how you feel about Luke."

How did she feel about Luke? At this point, she had absolutely no idea!

"I'm in love with Daniel, Barb. That hasn't changed." This was a dodge and she didn't care.

"I have a theory about being in love," Barb said after she took a small sip of tea. "Being in love is a dynamic experience. One that requires interaction between people. A living thing, if you will. I know how much you love Daniel. I know how much you will always love

Daniel. But my dear boy is gone, God rest his soul. And you—" Barb looked at her with steady, wise eyes "—are here. Among the living. You have a heart. You have needs. And there's absolutely nothing wrong with that! It takes two people to be in love. You love Daniel, yes. But you are 'in love' with Luke."

"I'm not *in love* with Luke," Sophia denied quickly.

"Oh, my dear. I beg to differ. I've been watching the two of you ever since I returned home. I believe that you return Luke's feelings. Perhaps you don't want to. Perhaps you think it's inappropriate...."

"To say the least!"

"But you love him nonetheless."

Instead of denying it again, Sophia took a different approach. "And you approve? Is that what you're saying? I'm pregnant with Daniel's baby and you are giving me the green light to date your other son? Don't you think that's a little..."

"Modern?" Barb asked with a mischievous smile.

"*Bizarre* is more the word I was searching for."

Barb's demeanor took on a more serious affect. "I don't think it's bizarre at all. If you ask me, it's the best thing that could happen to my family. Yes, I've lost one of my boys, and I will miss him for the rest of my life, but Luke is still here. He's alive. And he deserves to find happiness with the woman he has always loved." Barb's hand was on her arm again. "Daniel would approve. Daniel would want Luke to raise his son. How could that be wrong, or *bizarre,* as you put it? How could it be anything but wonderful, if God wills it?"

"And you don't think the rest of the family would object? Hank? He wouldn't object?" Sophia asked, and then added quickly, "Not that I'm saying anything is going to happen between Luke and me…I'm just curious."

"Everyone loves you. Everyone loves Luke. It's a match the entire family would get behind."

It took several minutes for Barb's words to sink in, but when they did, Sophia felt more confused than ever. She rubbed her temples with her fingertips. "My head aches."

Barb reached out. "Here. Let me have your hand."

Sophia stopped rubbing her head and extended her hand to her mother-in-law. Barb gave her fingers a reassuring squeeze. "Dear Sophia. I have loved you since the day Daniel first brought you home. You know that, don't you?"

Sophia nodded.

"You trust me not to lead you astray, don't you?"

Again Sophia nodded.

"Good! Then listen to me now. You're so young! You have so much living to do. Don't throw away happiness with both hands just because you think the timing is wrong. Life isn't like that. You have to go for it when you can! Grab the brass ring and don't let go. Luke loves you. He's a one-woman man, and you are *that* woman. You have always been that woman. And whether you believe it or not, Luke is the romantic one out of my twin boys. Not Daniel. Once he gives his heart away, there's no turning back. Why do you think he's been single all of these years?" Barb gave her fingers another squeeze. "His heart belongs to you, Sophia. And if I'm correct and you have given your heart to him, the only advice I can give you is go for it. Go for it, Sophia, and never look back!"

Chapter Twelve

The conversation with Barb had sent Sophia reeling. She retreated back to her bedroom to get her head screwed on straight. She tried everything to calm herself down, to make sense of what had just happened to her. Nothing worked. She paced, she tried to meditate and she took a hot bath. None of it helped; she felt as if a sinkhole had just opened and swallowed up her life. She couldn't seem to wrap her head around what had just happened to her.

Luke *loved* her.

"And Daniel knew."

All she could do was sit in the window seat, stare out at the driveway, and wait for Luke to return home from the airport. The minute he got home, they were going to have it out. Her shock had long since turned to anger.

How could she have been so blind?

How could she have been so *naive?*

All those years of fighting and bickering and Luke treating her like a second-class citizen had been a facade to protect himself. He had tortured her for years with his surly attitude and his "not so quiet" disapproval of her. It had all been a lie to cover his tracks!

She didn't know how long she waited impatiently on the window seat for Luke to return, but it was long enough that her backside was numb.

Finally, *finally* she saw the truck turn up the drive. She sprang into action and headed downstairs.

She poked her head into the kitchen. "They're here."

Startled, Barb turned quickly, her face bright with anticipation. "They're here?"

Sophia nodded as she pulled on her coat. She could barely get the thing buttoned over her bulging belly, but after a minute of struggle and cursing under her breath, the button hooked.

Barb knocked on her husband's study door. "Henry! Come on. They're here!"

Sophia opened the door, ignored the sharp, cold air that blasted in her face, and stood at the edge of the porch stairs. As the truck pulled up, she could see Luke in the front seat. His eyes were on her with that same intense look he always gave her. Armed with her new information, that look made perfect sense. He was looking at the woman he loved: her.

Hank and Barb emerged from the house, and they all walked down the drive together. Tyler, Luke and Jordan piled out of the truck.

"Where's Josephine?" Barb asked.

"Hi, Mom." Jordan threw her arms around her mother.

Barb hugged her daughter tightly. "Hi, my beauty!" Barb kissed her on the cheek and then asked again,

"Where's Josephine? Don't tell me she missed her flight!"

Jordan was hugging her father now.

Tyler spoke up. "She isn't coming, Mom."

"What do you mean, she isn't coming? Why not?"

Jordan had her head buried against Hank's chest. She turned her head slightly and said, "She's protesting the war."

"Protesting the war?" Each word was enunciated precisely. "What does that mean exactly?"

Jordan untangled herself from her father and made her way to Sophia. "She's not coming because Luke is a warmongering imperialist and her antiwar, peace-loving convictions won't allow her to stay in the same house with him."

Tyler raised his eyebrow at Jordan. "Is that a direct quote?"

Jordan shrugged nonchalantly. "I may have taken some creative liberties, but you guys got the gist, right?"

Barb was temporarily stunned speechless; Sophia had never actually seen that happen before. Then she snapped out of it. "Tyler, Henry, bring Jordan's bags, will you? I'm going to attend to this."

Without another word, Barb turned and disappeared through the front door. Sophia shook her head as she watched Barb disappear into the house. This was the last thing she would have expected from Josephine. It was the last thing that the Brand family needed at a time like this. What was normally levelheaded Josephine thinking?

"Wow, Soph! You're *huge!*" Jordan threw her arms around her and squeezed her tightly. Jordan leaned back and smiled broadly at her with straight, even, white teeth. "Still gorgeous, but *huge!*"

"Jesus, Jordan… Don't tell her that!" Tyler poked his head around the back of the truck.

"It's okay. I *am* huge." Sophia hugged her sister-in-law. Ever-blunt Jordan. A trait inherited directly from Barb.

Jordan put her hand on Sophia's belly. "So, when do you pop this little guy out?"

"Not soon enough." Sophia laughed. Jordan and she had always gotten along. Jordan was so much like Daniel: quick to smile, quick to laugh and always full of things to say.

Jordan dropped a quick kiss on Sophia's cheek before she headed into the house. "I'm freezing my butt off! Thank God I go to school in California!"

Tyler and Hank started to move toward the house, as well. "You coming?" Tyler asked her over his shoulder.

"Not yet," she said. Luke had headed to the barn soon after they had arrived. She couldn't have planned a more perfect opportunity. The two of them would be alone and the rest of the family would be occupied with Josephine.

Sophia found Luke at the other end of the barn chopping wood. His cane was propped up against the barn and he was hitting the wood in a way that let her know that he wasn't pleased with his sister's decision to stay in California.

Luke stopped his work for a minute and watched as she approached. His expression was neutral; no doubt he was wondering about her sudden appearance back in his life after days of avoiding him. When she looked back, her campaign to avoid him had been a childish thing to do.

"You shouldn't be out in the cold," he said as he wiped the sweat from his brow.

"You shouldn't try to boss me around."

She crossed her arms over her chest and stared him down through slightly narrowed eyes. Could this man really love her? It still didn't seem possible. It didn't seem likely or probable. She wouldn't believe it until she heard it from his lips, and his lips alone.

Luke straightened to his full height and gave her an expression she could describe only as "fed up." "Is there something you want, Sophia? Or did you just come out here to pick another fight with me?"

Sophia closed the distance between them, but stood off to the side as Luke swung the ax down and slammed it into the wood.

"We need to talk," she said bluntly.

Luke swung the ax again. "So talk."

Suddenly all the words that had been throbbing in her brain jammed up behind her lips and she couldn't say a word. She stood there and watched him swing the ax again and again while she tried to figure out how to begin.

Where was her righteous indignation? Where was her moral outrage?

Both had abandoned her, right at the very moment she needed them the most!

Finally, she pulled the letter out of her pocket and held it out to him. "I found this today."

"What is it?" He didn't bother to look at her.

"A letter you wrote to Daniel. About our engagement."

That got his attention. Luke jammed the ax into the wood and took a step toward her. His face was stony. "What did you find again?"

"You heard me," she said firmly as she waved the

letter in the air. "This letter says that you love me. Is that true?"

Luke looked around to see who might be within ear-shot before he walked over to her. He took the letter, glanced at it quickly before he stuffed it into his coat pocket. Then he wrapped his fingers around her wrist and began to walk toward the interior of the barn.

"Where are we going?" she asked and tugged at her arm. It didn't hurt; she just didn't like him leading her around like a pet. He immediately let go and they both stopped.

"It's too cold out here for you. Your lips are blue."

"What does that have to do with whether or not you love me?"

His eyes swept her face, and rested on her trembling lips. "You figure it out."

Luke continued to walk, but she refused to budge.

He stopped and turned. "Are you coming?"

She didn't like the authoritative tone he was using. So she snapped back, "Are you going to answer my question?"

Luke swept his hand toward the office. "Get out of the cold and I'll answer any damn question you have, Soph. Okay?"

"Fine." Grudgingly Sophia followed him to the heated office. In all honesty, although she didn't want to let on to Luke, she was actually grateful to get out of the cold. Boston was cold during the winter, but this was a different kind of cold. This was the type of cold that chilled your bones until they felt as if they were about to crack.

Luke held the door open for her. "You always have to have the last word, don't you?"

Sophia eyed him as she walked through the door. "I

could say the *exact* same thing about you, Brand." The warm air from the heater blasted her face and, almost instantly, the winter wear she was bundled up in seemed oppressive. "In fact, I *will* say the same about you!"

Luke shut the door firmly behind him. He yanked off his gloves and tossed them onto the desk. "I don't remember you giving Dan this much of a hard time."

"Daniel didn't spend every single one of his waking moments trying to think up reasons to antagonize me," Sophia snapped. She stood in one spot and didn't remove her outerwear, even though she was starting to sweat profusely under her arms.

"Dan was a saint," Luke said easily.

"Compared to you," she retorted.

Luke shrugged out of his coat and pulled the cap off his head before he closed the short distance between them. As he approached, her heart started to thud in her chest; deeper, harder, longer beats.

"You've got that straight, sweetheart," he said in that gravelly, suggestive voice of his. "Dan was the good twin."

Her stomach clenched when he reached out and unwrapped the scarf from her neck. It was a possessive move that she should have stopped, and yet…she didn't.

Her scarf joined his gloves on the desk. He reached out and began to unbutton her coat, his eyes locked with hers. He was giving her that hungry, restless, possessive look she had seen in his eyes before; she couldn't look away. She didn't want to look away.

One after another, Luke popped the buttons loose on her coat. When he reached the last one, he circled behind her and slipped it off her shoulders. When he pulled her wool hat off her head, the trance was broken and her temper flared.

"Hey! You don't have the right to manhandle me, Brand!"

Luke dumped the rest of her stuff on the desk. "Jesus, woman! Why are you so dramatic? You haven't seen manhandling."

Sophia cocked a brow at him. She had the distinct feeling that Luke could show her a thing or two about manhandling should she ever ask. A pleasurable kind of manhandling.

She shook her head at him. "You're stalling."

Luke leaned back against the desk and crossed his arms over his chest. The Marine mask was firmly in place. "What is it you want to know?"

A blush of embarrassment and anger stained her neck. She could feel the heat rush into her cheeks as she put her hands on her hips. "Do...you...love...me!"

"Friends love each other, don't they? And that's all we are to each other, right? Just friends?"

"That's not an answer, and you know it!"

"Perhaps it's not the answer you wanted, but it's the answer you got."

"It's not good enough."

"I don't know what to tell you," Luke said with a shrug. "It's the only one you're gonna get."

This time Sophia stepped closer. "Barb said that you're in love with me. She says that you've *always* been in love with me. Is. That. True?"

Luke's jaw clenched. A small crack in the mask. "Mom needs to learn to mind her own damned business."

"Be that as it may. Is it *true?* Is it?" Sophia threw up her hands. "Well? Is it? God, Luke, just *answer* the question! Do you love me?"

Luke looked off to the side for a minute while she

waited. She waited to the count of ten rapid heartbeats in her own chest before he looked back at her and simply said, "Yes."

He said it so bluntly, so starkly, without any fanfare or emotion, that it caught her completely off guard. "Yes?" she repeated for no reason at all. Her heart slammed into overdrive and she felt the blood drain from her face.

Luke saw Sophia sway to the left, saw the color drain from her face, and he was immediately at her side. He steadied her with both of his hands on her shoulders. "Take it easy," he said gently.

Truth be told, Sophia wasn't the only one having a physical reaction to the conversation. Luke felt a little sick himself. For the first time in ten years, he didn't have to hide his feelings from Sophia. It was a relief that he never expected to have. But that relief was overshadowed by fear. The idea of her limiting his contact with her son because it was too awkward between them was tearing him up inside. He knew he could never have Sophia; she would always look at him as a runner-up to Dan. But the boy? He couldn't stand the thought of losing him.

Sophia opened her eyes once she felt the dizziness pass. She brushed Luke's hands off her shoulders and moved over to the other side of the small room. Her mind was racing and she didn't know exactly what she wanted to say. There was a tense silence in the room as they both contemplated each other.

Finally, she said, "You love me?"

The mask was back. "That's what I said." Short, clipped, unemotional.

"You've been in love with me for ten years?" she elaborated. "Since college?"

"What is it about the answer 'yes' that's confusing you?"

Sophia's temper flared again. She waved her finger in the air. "Don't you get sarcastic with me, Luke. I'm not the one who sprang all of this on you when you are nearly nine months pregnant! I have a right to ask a few questions."

"Technically, you couldn't spring anything on me when I'm nearly nine months pregnant because I'm not a chick. I don't have a womb. Or ovaries for that matter, so…"

"Zip it, Brand!" Sophia interrupted him. She started to pace. Periodically, she glanced at him as she moved back and forth in the small room. "I'm pregnant, my husband is gone! I'm stuck in Montana, away from my business, my friends and my life." She stopped pacing to emphasize her words; she pointed to her chest. "And now I find out that, although you have acted like you couldn't stand me for the last ten years, you have actually been in love with me for ten years. I believe I've earned the right to ask a few questions!"

"Fine."

"You're damn right it's fine!"

"So ask," Luke said.

"I will!" Sophia started to pace again. When it was time to ask a question, she stopped. "When exactly did all of this 'falling in love' take place?"

She sounded like a prosecuting attorney grilling the defense's star witness. She didn't care.

Luke pushed away from the desk. "Before I answer any questions, I want you to promise me something."

"I'm not promising anything at this point," Sophia said angrily.

"Then this conversation is over." Luke turned around and grabbed her coat.

"Fine!" Sophia snapped. She knew Luke well enough to know that he would clam up in a heartbeat and never answer her questions. And she wanted answers to those questions. She needed answers to those questions. "What do you want?"

Luke kept the coat in his hands. "I want you to promise me that no matter what I say…no matter how you *feel* about what I say…you won't take that baby away from me."

Sophia felt as if Luke had physically slapped her. She was quiet for a split second before she said, "I wouldn't ever do that to you. Is that what you think of me?"

"Just promise," he demanded. She heard pent-up emotion resonating in his voice. It hit her that Luke was truly worried about losing his nephew, and her heart went out to him.

"I promise you, Luke. Of course, I promise. You are the closest thing my son will ever have to his father. I would be crazy to keep the two of you apart," she said firmly. "And I'm not crazy."

Luke accepted her answer and dropped her coat back onto the desk.

Satisfied, Luke answered the question. "I fell in love with you the minute I saw you." Luke was looking over her shoulder.

"When? The day Daniel introduced you to me?" Sophia tried to recall that moment, tried to remember the look in Luke's eyes. But she could only faintly remember Luke because she had been so wild about Daniel. All of her focus had been on him.

"No." Luke's lip raised in a faint smile. "Not that

day." He ran his hands over his cropped hair and sighed. "I fell in love with you weeks before."

Sophia shook her head. "What are you talking about? I'd never met you before that day."

"You hadn't met me. But I had seen you."

"Where?"

"Nordstrom's Department Store."

"Nordstrom's Department…" Her voice trailed off. She had worked at Nordstrom's in the fragrance department all through college and graduate school. She rubbed her temples; her head was throbbing.

There was nothing left to lose as far as Luke was concerned, so he added, "You were talking to a customer. The minute I saw you, I stopped in my tracks. You laughed at something, and I fell in love with you on the spot. I'd never seen anyone in my life as gorgeous as you. I still haven't."

Her legs felt heavy. She sat down in a chair and tried to process what she had just heard. After a minute, she shook her head and said, "But, if that's true, why didn't you come up to me? You never hesitate to go after what you want."

"You were working."

"You could have waited."

"You don't think I haven't been kicking myself about that for ten years? If I had just waited, you would have been mine. Mine. Not Dan's. Mine!" Luke hit himself once on the chest. "But I couldn't wait. I had a meeting with a recruiter, and I couldn't be late."

"You didn't come back for me." There was an accusation in her tone.

Luke's eyes darkened. "Like hell I didn't!"

Sophia had been staring at her wedding ring. She lifted her eyes to meet his. "When?"

"The next morning. You were gone. The lady you worked with told me you had a family emergency, that you wouldn't be back for several weeks. She gave out entirely too much information about you, but that's beside the point."

"That's when Grandpa died…."

"I suppose." Luke sat down in the desk chair so Sophia could look at him without craning her neck.

"I met Daniel when I got back," Sophia said softly, as much to herself as to Luke. "Are you telling me that this was some bizarre cosmic coincidence? You fall in love with me, and then two weeks later I fall in love with your twin brother?"

This wasn't a line of questioning Luke wanted to pursue. There were parts of this story that he'd rather leave unsaid.

Sophia noticed Luke's hesitation and prodded him. "Well?"

Luke took a deep breath in, and let it out in a long, slow, measured breath. "No. It wasn't a bizarre, cosmic coincidence."

"Then, what was it?"

"It was Dan being Dan."

"What's that supposed to mean?"

"Like you said, Dan didn't have a mean bone in his body. But he was a practical joker. And I was his favorite target."

"What does that have to do with me?"

"I told him about you."

"And?" Sophia started to feel queasy. She didn't like where any of this was going, but she couldn't stop herself from going there.

Luke leaned back in his chair and met her eyes head-on. "Dan thought it would be funny to beat me to the punch. Ask you out first."

Luke's words hit her like a swift kick to the gut. Her nausea worsened. She felt tears well up in her eyes, and spill out onto her cheeks. She swiped them away.

"Are you telling me—" rage was thick in her tone "—that I was a *joke* to Daniel?"

Her answer was written all over Luke's face. Enraged, she levered herself up. Once she stood up, she tried to step around Luke to get to the door. Luke sprang into action, grabbed her firmly by the shoulders, spun her around to face him and held on to her arms. "Don't leave here thinking the worst of Dan. He doesn't deserve that."

"He doesn't deserve it? *I* don't deserve *this!* To find out that the last ten years of my life has been based on a joke! My marriage..." She looked down at her belly. "My baby..." She glared up at him. "Why didn't you stop it? If you were so in love with me, why did you let it go on?"

"You're a smart woman. Why do you think?"

"I don't know!" she shouted at him and tried to wiggle away from his grasp. "Let me go!"

"No. I'm not going to let you go. Not *this* time!" Luke held on to her. "Dammit, Sophia! He fell in love with you. Don't you get it? Dan fell in love with you!" Luke's hands left her arms to cup her face. "He took one look at you and he saw everything I saw. You're so damned beautiful. You're smart, funny, kind. You're so *good* to everyone around you. Why wouldn't he fall in love with you? He would have been a fool not to!"

Sophia couldn't speak, but she didn't try to pull away. Luke's hands moved from her face to her hair, and then down to her neck.

"When he told me he was in love with you, I didn't give a damn. I wanted you for myself. But then I saw you with him. When I saw that you were in love with him…"

"You let Daniel have me."

His hands traveled from the nape of her neck back to her shoulders. The warmth of his hands was replaced by a rush of cold air, which brought with it an undeniable sense of loss.

"Daniel already had you. There wasn't anything I could do about it." Luke dropped his hands to his sides as the silence stretched out between them.

Sophia whispered, "So…I could have been married to you."

Luke said firmly, "I wouldn't have stopped pursuing you until I'd caught you. Until you were mine."

"And this baby could have been yours, not Daniel's."

"That baby is mine." His hand went possessively to her stomach.

"I mean, *really* yours."

Luke's eyes raked over her body; his gaze was undeniably predatory and sensual. "Make no mistake about it, Sophia. If you had been mine, I would have been making love to you every chance I got."

Chapter Thirteen

His hand was still on her stomach, and his lips were so close to hers that she could feel the warmth of his breath on her skin. Every fiber in her being wanted him to engulf her into his arms and kiss her senseless. But her brain wouldn't cooperate.

"I need to get back." She stepped away from him.

Luke stepped back as well and jammed his hands into the pocket of his jeans. He didn't say a word; his eyes were guarded. Silently, Luke helped her into her coat before he put on his. Then he said, "I'll walk you back."

"That's not necessary." This was said quickly.

"I'll walk you back," he repeated quietly, firmly. She could tell by his tone that he wasn't going to take no for an answer.

Sophia nodded. She was being ridiculous. "You're probably right." No sense letting her pride and discomfort put her at risk for slipping on a patch of ice this late in her pregnancy.

As they made their way through the barn, Sophia glanced at Luke from the corner of her eye. Every once in a while, she would see him wince. It was barely perceptible, but she saw it nonetheless.

"Why are you so stubborn about using your cane?"

Luke offered her his arm as they stepped into the snow. "The sooner I can walk without it, the sooner I get back to my men."

She felt sick at the thought of Luke going back to Afghanistan. Why in the world had she ever allowed herself to care about this man, when all he was going to do was put himself right back into harm's way? The last thing she needed was to bury another Brand man she loved.

Sophia stopped walking. The thought of losing Luke, the way she lost Daniel, had halted her in her tracks. She couldn't stand the thought of life without Luke. And in that moment, as that thought pinged through her brain, her muddied emotions began to crystallize. Out of the blue, it struck her like an electric shock. She truly did love Luke. Not as a platonic friend. She loved Luke as a man. And she was scared to death that she was going to lose him.

"What's wrong?" Luke stuck by her, loyal and dependable, just as Daniel had always said.

Sophia shook her head and didn't meet his gaze. She started to walk again, anxious now to get back to her room. She needed time to think; she needed time to figure out what to do. She just needed time....

The family was gathered in the kitchen and everyone was talking at once; the conversation was loud and raucous.

"I sent my daughter to college to get an education. I did *not* send her there to have left-wing liberal professors fill her head with their political agendas! And why, might I ask, isn't your daughter answering that very expensive phone we pay for every month?" Barb was talking while she rearranged the kitchen.

"Honey, will you please stop rearranging the kitchen every time you get upset? None of us can find anything once you're done," Hank asked in a beseeching tone that wasn't his norm.

Barb addressed her husband; she had a spatula in her hand. "This is how I cope. This is how I've *always* coped. In forty-three and three-quarter years of marriage, have I ever let you starve?" She didn't wait for him to answer. "No. I haven't. So, as far as I'm concerned, this is a perfectly acceptable way for me to work through my frustration. *And* until I give you some reason to complain about how I take care of you, I would appreciate it if you would kindly mind your own business when it comes to my kitchen!"

Hank relented easily. "Fair enough." He'd been married to Barb long enough to know when to back away.

"Mom." Jordan drew her mother's attention away from Hank. "I think this is more about Jo wanting to hang out with her boyfriend over the holidays than a war protest."

"Boyfriend?" Barbara and Hank asked in unison.

Tyler let out a long, low whistle. "The plot thickens."

"Not everything's a joke," Barb snapped at Tyler, whose grin only grew wider as he winked at Sophia.

"Why haven't I heard about a boyfriend before now?" Barb zeroed back in on Jordan. "What is going *on* with your sister?"

Jordan held up her hands. "Hey…don't put this on

me! Why do I always get the blame for every little thing Jo does? I'm not my sister's keeper...."

"This is payback, if you ask me," Tyler interjected.

"What's that supposed to mean?" Jordan demanded in an indignant tone.

"That means," Tyler explained, "that Jo is usually the one getting the third degree about all of the crap you're normally up to."

Jordan threw up her hands. "You know what? Instead of giving me the third degree about Jo, why don't you guys give me a little credit for being here? I'm the one who's scared to death of flying, and yet I showed up. Shouldn't I get some sort of praise for that?"

Undeterred by Jordan's comment, Barb continued with her line of questioning. "Obviously there's something wrong with this young man, or she wouldn't be hiding him from us. What does this boy do? Is he in school? How old is he?"

Jordan frowned. "Mom, you need to ask *her*. For once, I haven't done anything wrong, and I'm *still* the one on the chopping block. That's totally unfair!"

Barbara swiveled her head and looked at Luke. "What do you think about your sister's behavior?"

"I think that everyone handles grief in their own way, Mom. Dan was Jo's favorite—that's not a big secret. Maybe she just couldn't face Christmas here without him. Either way, it's up to Jo to explain herself."

"Thank you, Luke!" Jordan tipped her head back to look at her older brother. "Finally! The voice of reason!"

While the family was distracted by Josephine, Sophia slipped upstairs. She needed to be off on her own to sort things out. She needed solitude. Later she begged off dinner as well, not ready to leave the darkness and quiet of her room. She found herself retrieving one memory after another of her encounters with Luke. Finally his behavior toward her made perfect sense. But even if she had known about Luke's feelings for her, it wouldn't have changed anything. Her love for Daniel had been absolute. So, in the end, in the calm aftermath of reasonable thought, it made perfect sense for Daniel and Luke to keep this information from her. Still, now that she knew about Luke's feelings for her, what next? How would she act? How would they move on? That's what she needed to figure out, and on that front she didn't have a single answer. For once, she was truly going to live by Daniel's favorite motto and "go with the flow," see how things panned out.

Sometime later Sophia heard Luke enter his room. Her heart seized at the thought of him being so close, and then it started to thud steadily and strongly in her chest. Almost in an automated movement, she threw back the covers and turned on the bedside lamp. The light hurt her eyes and she covered them for a moment. Everything in her was being pulled to Luke's room. She didn't know what she would say, but she had an undeniable urge to see him. To touch him.

"And there is the truth of it," she said to herself softly. She couldn't deny the magnetic pull she felt whenever Luke was near.

She passed quietly through the bathroom and knocked lightly on the door. Without a word Luke opened the door and let her in. She sat down on the bed next to him, and for several minutes neither one of them spoke.

"Are you okay?" Ever the protector, Luke's concern was for her.

She nodded and reached out for his hand. "Are you?"

His thumb moved over her wedding band before he

gave her hand a squeeze. He left her on the bed and moved to a chair across the room from her. He sat down and began to remove his boots. "Honestly? I'm relieved. I've been carrying that around for a long time and I'm glad it's over."

Her stomach flip-flopped when he said "it's over." "You weren't going to tell me, were you?"

His boots made a thud as he dropped them next to the chair. "No."

"Not ever?"

He leaned back. "Not ever."

"Why not?"

"What would it have accomplished, other than make things more strained between us? I was trying to make things better, not worse. I'd never lay all of this on you when you are grieving and pregnant. Not my style. Honestly, I wish you hadn't found that letter, but what's done is done."

When she didn't say anything, he continued.

"Now that it's out in the open, I feel I can finally move on. I just hope you didn't get too beat up in the process."

"What if I don't want you to move on?" This was blurted out of her mouth before her brain had a chance to stop it.

The room became very still; neither one of them moved. She actually had to remind herself to take a breath while she waited for his response. It never came. He simply sat in the chair without moving an inch, and contemplated her as if she were a code to be deciphered. Humiliated, she finally said, "I don't know why I said that."

"You're all mixed up."

She couldn't argue with him. "Can we forget I said that?"

Luke stood up. "It's already forgotten." He walked over to her and held out his hand. He was being so gentle with her, so kind, that it made her heart break a little for the both of them. She slipped her hand into his, reveled in the strength and warmth of his fingers as they closed over hers.

He seemed so calm now; the tension that she had always sensed in him was released, and now she was left with a man who seemed to accept his fate. They had traded places. Now she was the tense one.

"I'm not going to apologize for loving you, Sophia." He took both of her hands in his and held them. She titled her head up and took in the rugged planes of his face.

"I don't expect you to."

"It never occurred to me that Dan and I would fall for the same woman—we never had before. But it happened, and I suppose the better man won."

She didn't know what to say, so she said nothing at all.

"I can live with loving you and not having you. That's how it's always been. I've become accustomed to it." He lifted his lip in a self-effacing half smile. She returned the smile. "But what I can't tolerate is being cut out of little Danny's life. That's my priority in all of this—it has been ever since I found out you were pregnant...."

"I already told you, Luke, I would never keep you from seeing him as much as you want. Nothing will ever change that, no matter what the future brings for either one of us."

"I know. And I believe you, Soph." Luke released

her hands and reached up to brush the hair away from her face. "I just don't want you to feel awkward around me because of all this. Okay? Let's just concentrate on you having a healthy baby."

As his hands dropped away from her face, she found that the feeling of loss was nearly unbearable. She ached to have Luke touch her again. She ached to be in his arms, but she had the distinct feeling that she would never feel his arms around her again. Not like before. He loved her, yes, but he had no intention of pursuing her. And that made her feel ridiculously rejected.

She rubbed her hands over her belly and nodded in agreement. "I was hoping he would arrive for Christmas. You know, like the best Christmas present ever?"

Luke guided her to the door; the meeting was over. "I hope that boy has the good sense not to show up on Christmas."

"Why not?"

"Kids who are born on Christmas always get screwed in the present department. Let the kid have his own day, at least."

"I hadn't thought of that, but you're right."

Luke held on to the door and leaned toward her slightly. "Are we good now?"

"Yes."

"I'd like for Mom to have the best Christmas she can have, considering..."

"We're good. Really. I wouldn't say it if I didn't mean it."

"I know that's right. Then we're square."

"Square." She smiled as she outlined a square shape with her fingers.

"Good night, Soph."

"Night."

"And keep that baby in there cooking until after the holiday!"

She smiled at him over her shoulder. "Easy for you to say, Brand! You're not the one lugging him around. I'm ready for him to come out on Christmas Day, or any other day for that matter!"

The next week leading up to Christmas raced by for Sophia. The Brand family always made a big deal about holidays, and even without Daniel and Josephine, Barb was determined to make it a merry Christmas. Sophia threw herself into the holiday spirit, doing her best to keep her mind off Luke. But the truth was, it was never far from her mind. Unfortunately, it seemed that his confession had given Luke a sense of ease with the situation, and he didn't seem bothered by her at all. It was as if the release of the secret had washed away the sexual tension that had been emanating from him. In fact, he was acting exactly like her platonic friend, and she should be happy about it. She should be thrilled! But she wasn't. The truth was that she hated it.

And she wanted him to stop it!

She wanted what they had before his family had returned. She wanted her Luke back. And the fact that he could so easily push aside his desire for her made her wonder if he really loved her, or if he had just been infatuated with a fantasy woman who didn't really exist.

In spite of herself, she had become somewhat of a visual stalker. Her eyes would seek Luke out wherever he was. She found that she enjoyed looking at him, enjoyed watching him as he interacted with his family. Of course, she rarely caught him looking back at her, and when he did meet her eyes, he gave her a mild, platonic nod that left her feeling completely dissatisfied.

Her head was saying it was a good thing; after the baby was born, she was going back to Boston. After his leg healed, Luke would go back to active duty. Their lives had intersected briefly at this point in time, but soon their paths would move apart. She had to accept that.

Unfortunately, her heart was having a hard time falling in line with her mind.

She had fallen for Luke; there wasn't any doubt in her mind about that anymore. But she would never be involved with a military man. She couldn't be. And Luke would never leave his career with the Marines. As far as she could see, there wasn't a future for them. Not as a couple. Why was it so hard for her to accept this when it seemed that Luke had already moved on?

Just after midnight New Year's morning, Sophia was alone in the family room watching the lights twinkle on the Christmas tree. The entire family had turned in after the stroke of midnight, even Jordan. She had thought to get up several times to turn in, but she found that she was almost too tired to get up. Nine months pregnant and everything was a chore; she was ready to have the baby and move on. It was a relief to know that if Danny didn't make an appearance of his own in one week, her doctor would induce labor. She was tired of feeling tired, and she hated the fact that she was waddling instead of walking. The thrill of being pregnant was beyond gone.

"I thought I was the only one still awake," Luke said from the doorway.

Sophia caught her breath. "You startled me."

"Want some company?"

"Of course." She patted the seat cushion next to her.

"I was just admiring the tree one last time. Your mom is obsessive about packing everything up on New Year's Day."

She had also been feeling sorry for herself, not that she would share this truth with Luke. But this was the first time since college she hadn't received a New Year's kiss. And if she had hoped that Luke would sweep her up into his arms for a New Year's kiss, that little fantasy of hers had been shattered into a thousand pieces. At the stroke of midnight, Luke had crossed the room to her, and he had kissed her cheek in the most annoyingly bland way.

Luke sat down next to her on the couch. "She has her routine, that's for sure."

They both sat in silence for several minutes and then Sophia heard Luke chuckle.

"What?" she asked.

Luke nodded toward the German shepherd sleeping in front of the waning fire. Ranger was draped across the large dog, sound asleep. "Even Elsa has succumbed to his persistence."

Sophia smiled as well. "He's irresistible."

"Yes, he is," Luke agreed, easily.

After a moment of silence Sophia turned her head toward Luke.

"I thought you had already turned in." Sophia admired his strong profile.

"I couldn't sleep."

"I couldn't get out of this couch!"

That got another chuckle out of Luke. After a minute she said, "I want to thank you for my present. I can't imagine how you arranged it."

"The military can be a small world."

She picked up Daniel's dog tags that she now wore

around her neck and held them tightly. "These are what I wanted the most. I still can't believe that I have them...."

"I'm glad you like them."

"I love them, Luke. I can't thank you enough. Really."

"No need to thank me. I was happy I could do it for you."

"I didn't have anything for you...."

Luke gave a quick shake of his head. "I have everything I need."

Those words hit her in the gut. After a pause, she asked, "Is that true? There isn't anything else that you need?"

Luke got up and put distance between them. Even in the sparse light, as he straightened after stoking the fire, she could see the tension in his jaw, the stiffness in his shoulders. "I don't need much."

"What about a family?"

Luke leaned against the mantel and crossed his arms over his chest. "I've got family."

"You don't have a wife." Why was she going down this path?

He didn't respond.

"You don't have children," she added belligerently.

Luke pushed away from the mantel. "What's this about, Sophia? What are you driving at?"

"I'm just having a friendly conversation." That was a lie.

"No, you're not." Luke didn't hesitate to call her on that lie. "You're trying to make a point, but I sure as hell don't know what it is."

"No point." She shrugged. "We can change the subject. We could talk about anything you'd like to talk about. Or we can talk about nothing at all."

"Bull," Luke said flatly. He dragged a chair over to the couch and sat facing her. "What's your angle, *friend*? Spit it out. What have I done *now*?"

The word *friend* hit her like a slap in the face; no doubt that was his intention. "Nothing. You haven't done anything." That was the problem. She was feeling neglected by him and she couldn't bring herself to say it. She wasn't going to go chasing after him like a schoolgirl begging for a second of his time.

Luke leaned forward and rested his arms on his thighs. All his attention, every fiber of his energy, was focused on her. "Dammit, Sophia. I can't seem to do anything right with you, can I? No matter how hard I try, I always fall short. I always disappoint you in some way. I always manage to *let you down*." He blew out a frustrated breath. "Just tell me what I'm doing wrong and I'll fix it. Okay? I'm like goddamned putty in your hands!" Then lower, almost to himself, he said, "That's how damned well pathetic I've become."

"You're not pathetic."

"I'll be the judge of that." He lifted up his head and even in the darkness she was held captive by his striking eyes. "What…have…I…*done*?"

Sophia suddenly felt weary. She felt weary of being pregnant, of dealing with Daniel's loss, of being in Montana, and she was especially weary of her feelings for Luke.

"It's not you, Luke. Honestly, it's not. It's me…."

"Bull."

"I'm being serious. My rotten mood doesn't have anything to do with you. All right? You've been perfect. You've kept your end of the bargain, okay? No complaints. I'm just fed up with feeling like a holiday parade float, and I want to go home. Neither of those things have anything to do with you." She reached out her hand. "Will you help me up, please? I'm ready to go to bed."

"Not a problem."

Luke held on to her hand as she slowly stood. She took a few extra moments to stand upright, and he could tell that she was feeling lousy. He wished he could do something to make her feel better, to ease her pain, but he knew that his hands were tied.

Luke slipped his arm around her shoulder and offered his other arm to Sophia for balance. She held on to Luke's arm gratefully, glad that no matter how irrationally she acted toward him, Luke never failed to offer her support. As Luke walked her to her room, his expression was both guarded and concerned. "Are you certain that I haven't done anything to upset you?"

Her shoulders dropped. She knew that this was all about him not losing touch with his nephew. That's what mattered to him, and she was grateful. But she felt invisible to him now, and that hurt.

"How about this… Ask me when I'm not nine months pregnant, okay? I have no doubt my answer will be a much different one." Her back was against her bedroom door and her hands were resting on her distended belly. "I did have something I wanted to ask you, though. It's something I've been thinking about, but you don't have to do it if you don't want to.…"

"What's that?"

"The doctor is inducing me next week. This boy is just getting too big for me."

"Mom told me." Luke took a step closer to her.

"Would you like to be in the room when Danny is born?"

At first Sophia thought that Luke might not have heard her. He stood stock-still, his expression devoid of emotion. She was about to repeat her question when Luke dragged her into his arms for a bear hug that temporarily cut off her breath. He hugged her tightly, then pressed a hard kiss on her cheek before he released her.

"I'd be honored," Luke said finally. In the dim light she could see that Luke's eyes were glassy with emotion.

"I'll be glad to have you there." She reached out and gave his hand one last squeeze.

"Happy New Year," Luke said before he opened his door.

"Happy New Year, Luke."

With that, they parted company, and as Sophia gently closed her door behind her, she felt a deep sadness sweep over her. Luke was still interested in her son; that was apparent. But he had disconnected himself from her. He had unplugged and stepped back; she felt as if she had lost her best friend. Somewhere along the line Luke had gotten under her skin, had become a part of who she was. And then, just as unexpectedly, he had slipped away from her.

Chapter Fourteen

Sophia tried everything she could to sleep, but it was no use. Danny had his foot jammed underneath her rib cage again; he could not be persuaded to move. And, to make matters worse, she couldn't get her earlier conversation with Luke out of her mind. It wasn't like her to play the wounded, wordless female to get out of sticky situations. And yet, that's what she had allowed herself to become. Instead of coming right out and saying what was on her mind when she had the opportunity, she had chickened out. She had lied. She had evaded. And now she couldn't sleep.

"That's it! If I'm awake, he might as well be awake, too." She slipped out of bed, threw on her robe and made her way to Luke's room. She didn't bother to knock. Instead, she gently opened the door and stepped inside. Luke was sprawled out on his back as he slept.

She reached out and shook his arm lightly. Luke's eyes immediately popped open.

"What's the matter? Is it the baby?"

Sophia shook her head. "No."

Luke propped himself up on his elbow. "What's the matter?" He repeated the question.

"You were right earlier. I am upset about something."

Luke took a deep breath in through his nose and looked at his watch on the nightstand. "It's three o'clock in the morning, Soph. Can't it keep?"

"No." She shook her head again. "I can't sleep."

"So I shouldn't sleep either? Is that it?"

"It sounds bad when you put it like that." She frowned.

"It sounds bad because it *is* bad." He stood up and yanked on his jeans. "But you're pregnant and you're a woman, so I guess you have the right."

"That was a real oinky thing to say."

"And your point is?" Luke raised a brow at her. But after a moment of thought he held up his hand. "Wait. Scratch that. Let's stay on track here. I may be a chauvinist…"

"You absolutely *are* a chauvinist…"

"But that's not why you're standing in my room in the middle of the night, correct? Or is it?"

"I don't think I like your tone.…"

"You don't like my tone?"

"No. I don't!" Irritation had already crept into her voice.

"Well then, I suppose we're even, sweetheart, because I sure as hell don't like the fact that you just woke me up out of a sound sleep because you're displeased with life in general."

"That's not true. I'm very happy with…"

Luke was at her side. He took her by the shoulders and guided her until she sat down on the bed. He held on to her. "Dammit, Sophia!" he said in a harsh whisper. "You're driving me bloody crazy. Do you understand that? Do you have any concept of it? You are the most annoying, infuriating, disagreeable, frustrating, *complicated* woman I have ever met. And, unfortunately, I love you for it, which makes me a complete nut job! Will you *please* tell me why you woke me up?" By the time he was done, he was no longer whispering.

"Shhhh! Keep your voice down!" she said in a loud whisper. "Someone will hear you."

"I don't give a damn if someone hears me."

"Well, I do! I don't like to have everyone in my business. It's already bad enough that…"

Luke snatched up his watch off the nightstand. "You have ten seconds to start talking."

"Quit bossing me around, Luke! I'm not one of your men. I don't worship the ground you walk on! I'm not mandated to follow every little word you say as if it's the holy gospel, and I'm not just going to jump because you order me to do it.…"

"Eight seconds. Seven. Six." He gave her a questioning look. "Five…"

"All right!" she whispered harshly and waved her hand. "All right! Put that stupid thing down."

"Talk." Luke sat down heavily in the chair and waited.

Sophia muttered, "I still don't like your tone."

"Sophia…"

"Or that you are speaking to me like I'm a toddler. I'm not a child!"

Luke went to stand up. "That's it…"

Sophia made a hand gesture for him to remain sitting. "Will you quit rushing me? You're always rushing me!"

"Pregnant or not, I'm gonna kick your butt right out of my room if you don't start talking. You've worn me out, woman…."

Sophia clasped her hands together; she knew that her stall tactics weren't working. It was time to come clean with Luke. So she did.

"You were right. I have been upset…."

"You mentioned that."

She glanced up at him; she had his unwavering attention. "I miss you."

"How can you miss me if I haven't gone anywhere? I'm right here."

She felt emotionally deflated and her body sank lower onto the mattress as her shoulders drooped. "You treat me differently now. I miss how things were between us before your family came back. I miss that."

She waited for him to respond, but he just sat there and stared at her. She added, "Your turn."

"I'm thinking," Luke said in a biting tone. Then, after a moment, he said, "You know, you're really pissing me off right now, and I really need to think about what I'm going to say because I don't want to fight with you."

"I don't want to fight with you either," she interrupted him. "And I wasn't trying to piss you off. Why are you pissed off?"

Luke rubbed his hands several times over his shorn hair and blew out a breath. "Because, Sophia," he said in a slow, measured voice, "I've done everything I can think of to make you happy, to make things right between us, to treat you how you want to be treated. I walk on goddamn eggshells all the frickin' time for you; I'm on pins and needles constantly for you, and yet… It's not enough. You're still not happy. You're still upset! What the *hell* do you want from me? Tell me now. What the hell do you *want* from me!"

"I want you, Luke," she said simply. Honestly. "That's what I want. You."

"You have me. You've always had me. Haven't you been paying attention these last couple of weeks?"

"Ever since the…barn…you've treated me like…" She paused to think of the right word. "Like we've never had anything between us. You avoid me like the plague, and when we do see each other, you do everything you can not to touch me. Don't think I haven't noticed, Luke, because I have."

These words moved Luke to action. He stood up and marched over to her. "I'm sorry. I don't think I heard you correctly. Have you woken me up in the middle of the night to complain about the fact that I don't *touch* you enough?"

"Yes." She felt like a lunatic.

"Unbelievable." Luke's eyes blazed with emotion. "You're unbelievable!"

Luke started to pace; his limp was barely noticeable now. He paused for a moment and addressed her. "Let me get this straight. You've been trying to get me to treat you like we're 'just friends' since the moment I arrived here, and now that I'm finally complying with *your* wishes and demands, you…don't…like…it?" His tone was incredulous. "You have gotten everything *your way,* and you still aren't happy? This is priceless! And you wonder why I'm a chauvinist! Women are nuts!"

She supposed he had a right to be a little caustic at this point. She *was* acting nuts. "I admit that in the beginning, that's what I wanted. But, honestly, I think that

I was just trying to push you away because I was afraid of how I was feeling about you…."

"Jesus, woman! Will you lay off the frickin' psycho-babble for one second, please?"

"Understanding the psychological motivation behind our actions is the cornerstone of change," Sophia said with a lift of her chin. "Plus, it's my profession. Analyzing emotions is my stock-in-trade."

Luke looked up at the ceiling, lifted his hands in the air and said, "Shoot me now, Lord. Just shoot me now!"

Not deterred, Sophia continued. "I just want to know why you're treating me like you don't have any feelings for me at all! Why are you pushing me away?"

"Why am I pushing you away?"

"Yes."

"Why am I pushing you away?" he asked again, loudly.

"Shhhh." She lowered her voice to a whisper. "Yes, Luke. Why are you pushing me away?"

"You know what, Sophia? I'm flat-out tired of all of this crap with you. You want to know why I'm pushing you away? Fine! I'll tell you. Why not? What do I have to lose? I'm treating you like a *friend* to keep myself in check, you get it? I treat you like a friend who's off-limits so I don't cross the line. You should be thanking me instead of sitting here busting my balls about it!"

"Cross what line?"

"You're the shrink. You figure it out."

"I want to hear it from you."

Luke crossed the room to her and pulled her gently to a stand. His fingers were in her hair as he tilted her head so they were gazing into each other's eyes. She could see that Luke was warring within himself; he was very close to kissing her, and she was very close to letting him. Instead, he said, "I've wanted you for ten years. *Ten years.* That's a hell of a lot of pent-up desire, woman. I want you all the time, get it? Whenever I see you, I want to put my hands on you. Put my hands all over you. You're just so damn sexy and you think I should be turned off because you're pregnant. But you're sexy as hell like this, too. You drive me nuts, do you get that? I have to fight not to strip you down and put my lips on every damn inch of your body. Do you hear what I'm saying to you, Sophia? I want you so much it hurts. I want you in my bed. Naked. All the time. I want to be able to touch you whenever I damn well please. I want to kiss you whenever I damn well please. This is what you do to me." Luke pressed himself against her, and there was no mistaking that he was aroused. Luke watched as realization dawned in her eyes before he spoke again. "*That*—" and they both knew what *that* was "—is why I have a strict *hands-off* policy with you, Sophia. Are we clear now?" He stepped away from her. "Because if I don't keep a barrier between us, I'll take advantage of your confusion and make love to you every damn chance I get. I'll talk you out of your clothes and into my bed before you know what hit you!" His voice lowered to a lover's caress. "Don't think I can't."

Luke's eyes dropped down to her lips. Speechless, she licked them involuntarily. She cleared her throat and tried to keep herself focused on the conversation. He was making it nearly impossible to think, much less form a coherent sentence. "And then everything would be ruined."

"What?" His eyes drifted back up to hers.

"You're afraid that you'll take advantage of me, we'll

make love and then in the morning, I'll regret it and everything will be ruined with Danny."

"That's part of it," he said in a quiet, husky voice.

"What's the other part?"

"You just can't leave well enough alone, can you? You just keep pushing and pushing...."

"This conversation had to happen."

Luke stared at her for several heartbeats; resignation flickered in his eyes just before he spoke. "I'm in love with you, Sophia. What part of that don't you understand? Do you think because I'm a man, that I'm a marine, I don't have any feelings? Do you think I like the fact that the woman I love, the woman I've *always* loved, doesn't love me back? I'm protecting myself from how I feel about you, because for me it's a matter of survival. I didn't know your permission was required."

Sophia put her hand on his arm. "Luke, you don't have to protect yourself from me. I'm not trying to hurt you."

"You can't help yourself." He pulled away from her.

His gesture stung, but it didn't deter her. She continued even though he had his back turned to her. "I don't know when it happened, but somewhere along the way, sometime during the week we spent alone, I fell in love with you, Luke."

If she thought that he was going to take her in his arms and hug her when he heard those words, she was sadly mistaken. Luke slowly spun around and looked at her. That stony mask was back in place, but his eyes were flashing with pent-up rage.

"Get out of my room," Luke bit out through gritted teeth and pointed to the door.

"Didn't you hear what I said? I'm in love with you." She said it more clearly, more decisively.

"I heard you," he snapped. "Now get out!"

"You stand there and tell me that I'm never going to love you back. I'm telling you that I'm in love with you, and now you're kicking me out?"

"Do you think that this is a game? A joke? You're not in love with me. You're in love with Dan! You always have been—no doubt you always will be. And I am not going to be some cheap substitution for my own twin. Do you hear me? I'm not going to be some pathetic second string that's suddenly in the game now because the first string got annihilated! I may be a lot of things, Sophia, but I sure as hell ain't no runner-up to Dan!" Luke's fists were balled up at his sides. "I'm nobody's stand-in."

"Is that what you think? That I want you to be a stand-in for Daniel? That's not it at all, Luke. I love Daniel, but…"

"I'm aware of that," he snapped.

"Will you let me finish, please?"

"Go ahead."

"I'll always love Daniel…."

"Do you think this is news to me or something, sweetheart? 'Cause it ain't," Luke interrupted her again.

"Dammit, Luke! Stop interrupting me. I'm trying to tell you that I'm in love with you. Do you get that, Captain Brand? I'm in love with you! Not Daniel. I love him. I always will, but as your mom put it so eloquently, 'being in love is for the living.' She's right. Being in love *is* for the living, and I'm in love with *you*."

"You're in no condition to know how you feel, Sophia. I look like Dan, you're confused, nothing more. And I'm not about to put myself in a position to have you wake up to that fact one month, two months, one year down the road. I'm not going to put myself out there like that. I'm not going to set myself up for that kind of fall. Do you hear me?"

"First of all, you don't even look that much like Daniel. I can't imagine why I ever thought you did. Your nose has that crooked thing going on, you have that scar on your jaw…" She reached up and traced the jagged white scar. "Probably from a bar fight, knowing you. *And* your eyes are a darker shade of blue with gold flecks around the iris. Second of all, I'd appreciate it if you'd quit throwing my pregnancy in my face! I'm pregnant, not brain-dead. I know my own mind, Luke…."

"Do you?"

"Yes! And I know my own heart. I'm in love with you. If you choose not to believe it, that's your problem. Not mine. The ball's in your court now."

Luke grabbed her left hand and held it up between them. "If you're so in love with me, why do you still have your wedding ring on?"

Sophia waited a minute for Luke to focus in on her finger and see that the wedding ring had been removed. Luke was so accustomed to being right, she truly enjoyed watching as it dawned on him that he was wrong.

Luke sought out her eyes. "When did you take it off?"

"Yesterday." She reached up and rested her hand on his face. "How can I wear Daniel's wedding ring when I'm in love with you? It would be a lie, and I'm not a liar."

Luke spun her around so her back was against the bedroom door. He placed his hands on each side of her, trapped her between his arms. His stormy blue eyes held her captive.

"You're in love with me?" Luke's lips were so close that his breath mingled with hers.

"Yes." Her voice had a soft, sensual quality; her knees felt weak. The scent of his warm skin was making her feel intoxicated.

Suddenly she was engulfed in his arms and his face was buried in her neck. She felt his lips on her skin, and the feel of his mouth on her flesh sent an electrical current racing through her body.

"I play for keeps," he growled as his lips found another spot on her neck. Her knees buckled and her pulse skyrocketed. Luke felt her sway; he held her closer and pressed himself against her possessively.

"So do I."

"I don't believe I gave you a proper New Year's kiss...."

Her heart was thumping in her chest. She licked her lips. "No. I don't believe you did."

Sophia closed her eyes as Luke's lips captured hers. She surrendered into his steely arms as Luke took possession of her mouth with his. Every nerve ending in her body ignited wherever his body touched hers.

"Do you have any idea how long I've waited to make you mine?" Luke abandoned her mouth as he reached for the belt on her robe and tugged it loose. He slowly opened her robe and slipped it off her shoulders. As it fell silently onto the ground at her feet, she felt completely exposed. Did he mean to make love to her right this minute? She was huge! She couldn't imagine it....

"Beautiful," Luke murmured. His eyes swept her body before they rejoined hers. "My God, you're gorgeous." He buried his nose back into her neck. "You smell so damned good, Soph." He brought his lips back to hers. "You taste so damned good."

"Luke...I don't think that we should..." She pushed

lightly on his chest; she felt overwhelmed by his passion for her.

Luke put his finger against her lips. "Shhhh. We aren't going to do anything that you don't want to do. I'm not going to hurt you or the baby." He moved his hand possessively down her body until his hand was on her belly. "But, my God, Sophia. I have to touch you. I have to taste you...."

She reached up for his face, relieved. "Yes. Yes." She said in a silken voice that she hardly recognized. "Yes."

Her last *yes* was cut off as his lips captured hers again. His fingers were in her hair, on her neck, down her back as he claimed her with his strong, unyielding lips. He kissed her again and again until she couldn't tell where his breath ended and hers began. She melted into his arms, felt herself let go of her well-constructed control, and kissed him back as forcefully as he was kissing her. She gave in to him, and claimed him in the very same way he was laying claim to her.

"Get in my bed," he growled against her lips.

His command was so masculine, so sensual, that she found herself complying without putting up her usual fight. She wanted to be in his bed. She wanted to be in his arms. She wanted to be his woman.

Once in his bed, she lay on her back feeling incredibly aroused, insecure and ridiculous. Her body was humming with desire and she was so horny she felt herself writhe on the bed; she needed a release that had been such a long time coming.

Luke's eyes never left her as he stripped out of his jeans. She could see the evidence of his desire for her straining against the thin material of his boxers. It was obvious that he wanted her as much as she wanted him.

He was at her side now; he pressed his body against

her. His fingers unbuttoned the buttons at the top of her nightgown. She sucked in her breath as his fingers slipped into her nightgown and cupped her full, warm breast. She arched her back against his hand, helpless to protest.

"Look at me." Luke hovered above her, his lips so close to hers as he spoke. "I want to make love to you, Sophia. Do you want me to love you?"

"Yes," she said without hesitation. "But look at me. I'm in no condition to make love. I'm huge. I feel ridiculous."

Luke's lips found the swell of her breast. "There are many ways for a man to satisfy a woman. All you have to do is let me…."

Sophia closed her eyes and moaned as his mouth moved to her nipple. As he began to suckle, she pressed her hand to the back of his head and moaned louder.

"Let me show you how much I love you…" Luke released her nipple.

She was squirming now, wanting, needing. "I need you, Luke. Please. I *need* you."

"Your wish is my command."

Luke's lips found hers as his hand slipped beneath her nightgown and traveled slowly up her thighs. "Open for me. Let me in," he said against her lips; after a moment she complied, relaxed as his fingers found her.

She reached down between them and slipped her hand into his boxers. Luke moaned her name into her neck as her fingers closed over his rock-hard erection.

He pulled her tightly toward him and grazed the skin of her neck with his teeth. "I've waited a lifetime for you, Sophia. A *lifetime*."

She couldn't speak. She couldn't respond. All she

could do was writhe against the warmth of his hand as he gave her the release that she had been craving.

"Luke." She gasped his name as she climaxed. "Luke."

"I love you, Sophia. God, I love you so damned much." Luke's words were groaned into her neck; his erection stiffened and then pulsated in her hand as he found his own release.

Chapter Fifteen

A week later the entire Brand family was gathered at the hospital to witness Sophia give birth to a healthy seven-pound, two-ounce baby boy. Luke and Barbara had been in the room for the birth while Hank, Tyler and Jordan kept themselves occupied with burned coffee and snacks from the vending machines. Luke held Sophia's hand during the delivery, cut the cord and, once Sophia had drifted off to sleep, made a beeline for the baby. Barbara stood arm in arm with her eldest son as they admired the latest addition to the Brand clan. "Just look at my first grandchild! He looks just like the two of you when you were born!" Barb said with pride. "He's the spitting image of his father *and* his uncle."

"He kind of looks like a raisin, if you ask me. Did Daniel and Luke look like raisins when they were born?" Jordan asked with a playful glint in her eye.

Barbara frowned at her youngest daughter. "Go find

your father, Jordy." That was her way of saying "beat it." Jordan took the hint and went off in search of Hank and Tyler.

Barbara squeezed Luke's arm; he shifted his gaze from his nephew to his mom. "It was wonderful for Sophia to let you be in the room. Daniel would have been so happy about that."

Luke covered her hand with his. "She did a good job, didn't she?"

"A fantastic job," Barbara agreed. "He's absolutely perfect."

Luke and his mother stood together and silently admired Daniel's son. Luke hadn't slept, but instead of resting, he watched little Danny; he couldn't seem to get enough. It was going to be tough to leave Sophia and her son when it was time to ship off to rehab. For the first time in his career, it was going to be tough to return to active duty. Luke believed that it was going to be the hardest thing he ever had to do in his life.

"I just wish that she would consider staying at the ranch with us. There are plenty of disturbed individuals in Montana who need counseling," Barb said. "I'm not going to name names, but there are *several* cookoo-noodles within a ten-mile radius of the ranch!"

"Mom... Don't bug her about it. She's been through a tough enough time without you laying a guilt trip on her. She's going back to Boston. Besides, seeing Danny will give you the perfect excuse to get back to the city."

Barb thought for a moment. "They do have very excellent shopping in Boston."

"There you go."

"Wonderful restaurants," Barb added.

"Dad'll hate it, you'll love it."

Barb chuckled. "Your father *will* absolutely hate it.

But he'll tag along just to see his grandson. And to make certain I don't melt my credit cards." Barb turned away from the window and faced her son. "Changing the subject, what is going on with Sophia and you? I've tried to keep out of it...."

"You've done amazingly well...."

"But enough is enough. What's going on with you two? Are the two of you going to raise Danny together?"

"We're not there yet, Mom."

"Why not?" Barb demanded. "It's not rocket science."

"Mom...stuff like this takes time. It's new to both of us. There's a lot to work out."

"Have the two of you already..." Barb lifted one suggestive brow. "You know..."

Luke looked down at his mom; a sense of absolute horror rolled around in his gut. "Have the two of us... what?"

"Oh, don't be obtuse, Luke! Have the two of you 'sealed the deal,' I believe your generation calls it...."

For the first time since he was a teenager, Luke felt the tips of his ears turn red with embarrassment. "Mom..."

"What?"

"You've crossed into a restricted area."

"Oh, please! I gave birth to you. I changed your diapers. I bathed you. I took your temperature with an anal thermometer! I don't have any *restricted areas* when it comes to my children."

"Well, you do now!"

Barb waved her hand and ignored his comment. "If you want my advice..."

"I'm not really in the market for it right now, so no..."

Barb's eyes sharpened, and it made Luke back down

a bit. "If you want my advice…" She started over again with very pointed, precise speech. "And you're going to get it whether you like it or not, because, no matter how old you are, I'm still your mother and you will always be my business.…"

"Yes, ma'am," Luke said respectfully.

Barb pulled out a small box from her purse and handed it to Luke. "I suggest you march right into that hospital room, get down on one knee and ask Sophia to marry you."

Luke cracked open the ring box and looked inside. "This is Grandma's engagement ring."

"Yes." Barb looked lovingly at the ring.

"Dan wanted to give this to Sophia when they were first engaged."

"I know," Barb said with her eyes still on the antique platinum-and-diamond ring. "I know he did. I just couldn't part with it then."

"But you can now?" Luke closed the lid of the box and slipped it into his pocket.

"Yes, I can. Perhaps that ring was always meant for Sophia." Barb's eyes drifted back to her grandson, who was stretching his legs and yawning. Her voice took on a poignant tone. "Don't let her slip away, Lucas. Seize this opportunity. This is *your* moment with Sophia. Don't let her go out of some false loyalty to Daniel. Daniel loved both of you and, as I have told Sophia, he would want the two of you to be together. He would want you to raise his son." Barbara sought out her son's eyes. "You do love her still, don't you, son?"

"More now than ever," Luke said without hesitation.

"Then, marry her, Lucas. Do whatever it takes to make her your wife, to make this boy your son." Barb squeezed her son's arm again and gave it a slight shake.

"This is your fork in the road, darling; we all come to them if we live long enough. Think hard and choose wisely, because you will never pass this way again."

Luke knocked lightly on the hospital room door before he opened it. At the sound of the door opening, Sophia opened her eyes and smiled weakly at Luke.

"Hi," she said softly.

Luke sat down in the seat next to the bed and took Sophia's outreached hand. "Hi. How are you feeling?"

"Probably a heck of a lot better than I look," Sophia said with a self-effacing chuckle.

"You look beautiful to me."

Sophia's eyes softened as she looked at him. "Thank you." She squeezed his hand. "Were you with him?"

Luke nodded. "I just came from seeing him. God, Sophia, he's incredible. Perfect."

"He is, isn't he? Barb showed me a baby picture of Daniel and you. Little Danny could be a triplet!"

Luke winked at her. "He's bound to be handsome."

"Bound to be." Sophia laughed before her expression turned more serious. "Listen, there's something I've been thinking about and I'd like to run it by you...."

"Shoot."

"I would like to name him Daniel Lucas Brand. How would you feel about that?"

Stunned temporarily speechless, Luke could only stare at the woman he loved. It never occurred to him that she would want to name her son after him; it was more than he could have ever hoped for. "Soph...you don't have to do that...."

She pushed herself up a bit in the bed. "But I want to. I can't imagine a better name for my son. Unless you'd rather I not..."

Luke pressed his lips hard against the back of her hand before he clasped it in both of his hands. "It's an honor that I never expected to have."

"So, it's okay with you?"

Luke leaned forward, pushed a tendril of hair behind her ear and then kissed her gently on her mouth. "Are you kidding? I'm blown away. I would love nothing more than to have your son carry my name. You're an amazing woman and I love you."

Sophia rested her palm against his stubbly cheek. "I love you, too, Luke."

Luke looked into her eyes as if he were trying to see into her soul. "I'm glad that you do, because there's something…" Luke began to reach into his pocket to pull out the ring box.

Sophia placed her hand on his chest, halting his words. "Oh! Hold that thought!" She had an excited sparkle in her eyes. "I have a Christmas present for you!"

"I told you I have everything I need…."

Sophia hit him on the arm playfully. "Quit spoiling this for me! I have the perfect gift for you!"

"You and Danny are the only gifts I need…."

Sophia made a frustrated noise and pointed. "*Please* go over to my pants and look in the pocket. I brought it with me for good luck."

Luke complied and searched Sophia's pockets. He pulled out a coin and examined it. He looked over to her, his teasing mood temporarily on hold. "This is Dan's Ranger coin."

"Merry Christmas!" Sophia said happily.

Luke came back to her bedside. "I can't accept this."

"Yes, you can. I want you to have it."

"You should hold on to this for Danny."

Sophia saw how Luke held the coin his brother had earned when he became a ranger with reverence. "I have a better idea. Why don't *you* hold on to it for him?"

Luke turned the coin over in his hand. "Are you sure?"

"Of course I am. Why wouldn't I be?"

Luke took one last look at the coin before he put it in his pocket and leaned over to kiss Sophia. "I don't know what to say other than thank you."

"You're welcome." Sophia wrapped her arms around Luke and hugged him tightly. "Thank you for being here with me, Luke. You made everything easier for me."

"This is where I was meant to be."

As Luke hugged Sophia, he thought about what his mother had said to him in the hospital corridor. This was his moment. This was his woman. He couldn't let her slip away from him a second time. Luke broke the hug, but held on to Sophia's hand. His heart began to pound hard in his chest at the thought of proposing to Sophia. He'd never proposed before, and he felt a wave of nerves and nausea hit him.

No matter what he had faced in combat, nothing compared with asking the woman he loved to be his wife. This was the most fear-producing mission he'd ever faced.

Sophia was eyeing him curiously. "I don't like your pallor, Luke. Have you eaten?"

"I'm not hungry. I'm nervous."

"Nervous!" Sophia said with a laugh. "When has Captain Luke Brand ever been nervous?"

"Right now."

Those words, along with Luke's serious demeanor, made Sophia's expression change from playful to one of concern. Now she felt nervous. "What's going on, Luke? You're scaring me. Are you leaving? Is that it?"

Luke grabbed her hands. "No. I'm not leaving. Not yet, anyway."

Sophia didn't like the "not yet" part, but she wasn't stupid. She knew she would be saying goodbye to Luke sooner or later.

"Then, what's going on?"

Luke pulled the ring box out of his pocket. "You had something in your pocket for me. And, as it turns out, I have something in my pocket for you…."

Sophia's eyes widened and her face drained of color. She couldn't take her eyes off the box in Luke's hand. "Luke…"

"Before you start psychoanalyzing the situation to death, could you just hear me out, please? Let me get through this uninterrupted. Can you do that for me?"

Sophia could only nod. Her tongue felt heavy and her mouth was suddenly dry; when she tried to swallow, her tongue stuck to the roof of her mouth, as if her saliva had turned to glue. She couldn't have gotten two words out if she had tried.

It never occurred to her that Luke might propose marriage; she was stunned. And completely unprepared.

Luke opened the box and held it out for Sophia to see. Sophia immediately recognized the ring and knew that there was only one person who could have given it to Luke: Barb.

"Sophia, I fell in love with you the minute I saw you, and I've loved you every day since. I never thought that I would have a second chance to make you mine, but now that I have it, I can't let you slip away. I have to try to make this work. I love you, Sophia, more than anything or anyone on this planet. I can't imagine my life without you in it; I don't want to imagine my life without you in it. I want you to be my wife, Sophia. I want to be your husband. I want us to live the rest of our lives together watching Danny grow." His eyes swept her body. "I want to watch you grow another child. Our child. I am going to love you until the day I die. I'm asking you to marry me, Sophia. I'm asking you to be my wife. Will you marry me?"

Unshed tears swam in Sophia's eyes as she looked between the ring and the man she loved. She couldn't seem to say a word, because she knew that the words she would say were going to hurt Luke. Luke's eyes were trained on her face; she could tell he was analyzing every flicker of emotion he read in her eyes. After a minute of silence, Luke sat back and snapped the lid of the box shut. Sophia jumped a bit at the noise the box made when it snapped shut. At the same time the box closed, Luke's expression became guarded.

She reached out for him instinctively. "Please, Luke...don't pull away from me, I..."

"You don't have to say anything to me, Sophia," Luke said in that unemotional tone he had picked up in the Marines. "Anything other than a 'yes' doesn't require an explanation."

Sophia felt her temper flare. "You ask me to marry you, and because I don't jump on the offer like some irrational, bubbleheaded teenager, you're going to shut me out? I'll explain myself if I bloody well want to, Brand, and you'll listen!"

Luke stood up, leaned against the windowsill and waited. "So, explain."

"Don't boss me around!" Sophia snapped. Luke could still get her blood boiling quicker than anyone else. After a moment, Sophia composed herself and said in a controlled, irritated tone. "You know, I didn't expect this—" she waved her hand between the two of them "—to happen."

"I didn't say you did."

"Can I please speak without you interrupting me? I didn't interrupt you."

Luke nodded his agreement.

"Thank you," she snapped. "Like I was saying, this thing between us is a complete shock to me. I didn't have any intention of falling in love with you. But I did. I love you, Luke. It's as much a surprise to me as it is to you, but there it is. And I won't regret it now. Loving you seems to be as natural as breathing for me." She clasped her hands together and rested them in her lap. "But let's be realistic, Luke. We're not kids anymore. We both know that it takes a lot more than love and a good romp in bed to make a marriage work."

"I'm aware of this."

"So am I. That's why, as much as I love you Luke, and I do…I really do, I can't be your wife. I can't stand the thought of marrying you and then losing you." The thought of Luke dying in combat overwhelmed her, and the tears she had been holding back slipped out of her eyes without her consent.

Luke was quick to offer her a tissue box. She pulled a tissue out roughly from the box and blew her nose loudly. "Thank you."

"So, let me get this straight… You won't marry me because of my career? That's the only thing holding you back?"

Sophia blew her nose again. "I just can't do it, Luke. I can't lose another husband like that." She balled the tissue up into her hand and gave him a disgruntled look. "As a matter of fact, it's actually pretty insensitive of you to ask me to marry another military man after what I've just lived through, don't you think?"

"I'd like to say something in own defense now, if you don't mind," Luke said.

Sophia nodded with a loud sniff.

"I made a decision last night. I'm not going to re-up, Soph. When my time is up, I'm leaving the Corps."

Sophia's heart started to flutter in her chest. "Are you serious? I can't let you do that…."

"It's not your choice. It's mine. I'm doing it for me. I'm doing it for us."

"I don't know what to say…."

Luke crossed to her side. He loomed over her, his handsome face tense; his eyes had darkened to a stormy midnight blue. "Say that you love me."

"I *do* love you, Luke. I'm crazy about you…."

Luke clasped her hand in his. "Then, be my wife, Sophia. Put me out of my misery and marry me! Nothing in this world matters to me more than you and Danny. I want us to be a family. Leaving the Marines isn't a big deal if you're the prize waiting for me at the end of that road." He pressed his lips to her hand; his eyes blazed with passion for her. "Say you'll *marry* me, Sophia."

"Yes." The word popped out of her mouth without a second thought.

"Yes?"

Sophia started to laugh. "Yes, Luke. God help me, I will marry you."

"I'd better get this on your finger quick before you change your mind or start to accuse me of being insensitive for proposing to you again." Luke pulled the box out of his pocket and slid the ring onto her finger. "I play for keeps, Sophia. You're never getting rid of me, no matter how angry I make you. No matter how many knock-down, drag-out fights we have, I'm never going to leave your side. Can you handle that?"

She wiggled her finger and watched the fire in the diamond reflect purple and blue and gold. "I can handle anything you throw at me, Captain. But are you really going to give up your career? For me?"

"For you. For me. For all of us."

Sophia reached up and put her hands on each side of his face; the flawless, colorless brilliant cut diamond winked at her as she said, "How could I be so lucky to fall madly in love twice in my life?"

Luke captured her mouth and kissed her breathless. "I'm the lucky one. I'm going to have a beautiful wife and a handsome new son. That's all I need. It's all I ever wanted…." He pressed his lips to the inside of her wrist. "Do you have any idea how much I love you?"

Sophia shook her head as Luke gathered her into his strong arms. She relaxed into his embrace with a contented sigh, just as a shiver of excitement raced up her spine when Luke's lips brushed against her earlobe. He whispered into her ear, "I'm going to show you for the rest of my life how much I love you, my beauty. Every day until I take my last breath."

Sophia smiled as he kissed the line of her jaw; she hugged him until her arms hurt. "You believe me, don't you?" Luke asked as he kissed the corner of her mouth.

"Yes," she said in a breathy voice. "I do."

"You'd better," Luke growled against her lips. Luke pulled her closer to him, molded her body tightly to his, as if he were afraid that she was going to disappear. Sophia pressed her lips to his, and held on to him as tightly as he was holding on to her. For the first time in a long time, Sophia felt safe. She felt secure. She was finally home. Wrapped up in his strong arms, Sophia knew that this loving embrace with Luke was going to last her a lifetime.

* * * * *

REQUEST YOUR FREE BOOKS!

2 FREE NOVELS PLUS 2 FREE GIFTS!

❧ Harlequin®

SPECIAL EDITION

Life, Love & Family

YES! Please send me 2 FREE Harlequin® Special Edition novels and my 2 FREE gifts (gifts are worth about $10). After receiving them, if I don't wish to receive any more books, I can return the shipping statement marked "cancel." If I don't cancel, I will receive 6 brand-new novels every month and be billed just $4.49 per book in the U.S. or $5.24 per book in Canada. That's a saving of at least 14% off the cover price! It's quite a bargain! Shipping and handling is just 50¢ per book in the U.S. and 75¢ per book in Canada.* I understand that accepting the 2 free books and gifts places me under no obligation to buy anything. I can always return a shipment and cancel at any time. Even if I never buy another book, the two free books and gifts are mine to keep forever.

235/335 HDN FEGF

Name	(PLEASE PRINT)

Address	Apt. #

City	State/Prov.	Zip/Postal Code

Signature (if under 18, a parent or guardian must sign)

Mail to the **Reader Service:**
IN U.S.A.: P.O. Box 1867, Buffalo, NY 14240-1867
IN CANADA: P.O. Box 609, Fort Erie, Ontario L2A 5X3

Not valid for current subscribers to Harlequin Special Edition books.

Want to try two free books from another line?
Call 1-800-873-8635 or visit www.ReaderService.com.

* Terms and prices subject to change without notice. Prices do not include applicable taxes. Sales tax applicable in N.Y. Canadian residents will be charged applicable taxes. Offer not valid in Quebec. This offer is limited to one order per household. All orders subject to credit approval. Credit or debit balances in a customer's account(s) may be offset by any other outstanding balance owed by or to the customer. Please allow 4 to 6 weeks for delivery. Offer available while quantities last.

Your Privacy—The Reader Service is committed to protecting your privacy. Our Privacy Policy is available online at www.ReaderService.com or upon request from the Reader Service.

We make a portion of our mailing list available to reputable third parties that offer products we believe may interest you. If you prefer that we not exchange your name with third parties, or if you wish to clarify or modify your communication preferences, please visit us at www.ReaderService.com/consumerschoice or write to us at Reader Service Preference Service, P.O. Box 9062, Buffalo, NY 14269. Include your complete name and address.

HSE11B

Turn the page for a preview of
THE OTHER SIDE OF US
by
Sarah Mayberry,

coming January 2013
from Harlequin® Superromance®.

PLUS, exciting changes are in the works!
Enjoy the same great stories in a longer format
and new look—beginning January 2013!

THE OTHER SIDE OF US
A brand-new novel
from Harlequin® Superromance® author
Sarah Mayberry

In recovery from a serious accident, Mackenzie Williams
is beating all the doctors' predictions. But she needs
single-minded focus. She doesn't *need the distraction*
of neighbors—especially good-looking ones
like Oliver Garrett!

MACKENZIE BREATHED DEEPLY to recover from the work-out. She'd pushed herself too far but she wanted to accelerate her rehabilitation. Still, she needed to lie down to combat the nausea and shaking muscles.

There was a knock on the front door. Who on earth would be visiting her on a Thursday morning? Probably a cold-calling salesperson.

She answered, but her pithy rejection died before she'd formed the first words.

The man on her doorstep was definitely not a cold caller. Nothing about this man was cold, from the auburn of his wavy hair to his brown eyes to his sensual mouth. Nothing cold about those broad shoulders, flat belly and lean hips, either.

"Hey," he said in a shiver-inducing baritone. "I'm Oliver Garrett. I moved in next door." His smile was so warm and vibrant it was almost offensive.

"Mackenzie Williams." Oh, no. Her legs were starting to

HSREXP1212HH

tremble, indicating they wouldn't hold up long. Any second now she would embarrass herself in front of this complete and very good-looking stranger.

"It's been years since I was down here." He seemed to settle in for a chat. "It doesn't look as though—"

"I have to go." Her stomach rolled as she shut the door. The last thing she registered was the look of shock on Oliver's face at her abrupt dismissal.

And somehow she knew their neighborly relations would be a lot cooler now.

Will Mackenzie be able to make it up to Oliver
for her rude introduction?
Find out in THE OTHER SIDE OF US
by Sarah Mayberry, available January 2013 from
Harlequin® Superromance®. PLUS, exciting changes are
in the works! Enjoy the same great stories in a longer
format and new look—beginning January 2013!